Cotton Mather, John W. Dean, Michael Wigglesworth, William H. Burr

The Day of Doom

Sixth Edition, 1715

.

Cotton Mather, John W. Dean, Michael Wigglesworth, William H. Burr

The Day of Doom
Sixth Edition, 1715

ISBN/EAN: 9783337389871

Printed in Europe, USA, Canada, Australia, Japan

Cover: Foto ©Andreas Hilbeck / pixelio.de

More available books at **www.hansebooks.com**

THE

𝕯𝕬𝖄 of 𝕯𝕺𝕺𝕸;

OR, A

POETICAL DESCRIPTION

OF THE

GREAT AND LAST

J U D G M E N T :

With Other Poems.

BY

MICHAEL WIGGLESWORTH, A. M.,

Teacher of the Church at Malden in New England,

1662.

ALSO A MEMOIR OF THE AUTHOR, AUTOBIOG-
RAPHY, AND SKETCH OF HIS FUNERAL
SERMON BY REV. COTTON
MATHER.

———

ACTS 17 : 31. Because he hath appointed a Day in the which he
will judge the World in Righteousness by that Man whom he hath
ordained.
MAT. 24 : 30. And then shall appear the sign of the Son of Man in
Heaven, and then shall all the tribes of the Earth mourn, and they
shall see the Son of Man coming in the clouds of Heaven with power
and great glory.

———

FROM THE SIXTH EDITION, 1715.

———

New York;
AMERICAN NEWS COMPANY.
1867.

C. S. WESTCOTT & Co., Printers, 79 John street.

MEMOIR OF THE AUTHOR.

THE following is the substance of an article published in the "New England Historical and Genealogical Register," for April, 1863, written by JOHN WARD DEAN, Esq., of Boston :

A century ago no poetry was more popular in New England than Wigglesworth's *Day of Doom.* Francis Jenks, Esq., in an article in the *Christian Examiner* for Nov., 1828, speaks of it as "a work which was taught our fathers with their catechisms, and which many an aged person with whom we are acquainted can still repeat, though they may not have met with a copy since they were in leading strings ; a work that was hawked about the country, printed on sheets like common ballads ; and, in fine, a work which fairly represents the prevailing theology of New England at the time it was written, and which Mather thought might, 'perhaps, find our children till the Day itself arrives.'"

The popularity of Wigglesworth dated from the appearance of his poem, and continued for more than a century. Expressing in earnest words the theology which they believed, and picturing in lively colors the terrors of the judgment day and the awful wrath of an offended God, it commended itself to those zealous Puritans, who had little taste for lofty rhyme or literary excellence. The imaginative youth devoured its horrors with avidity, and shuddered at its fierce denunciation of sin. In the darkness of night he saw its frightful forms arise, and was thus driven to seek the "ark of safety" from the

wrath of Jehovah. For the last century, however, the
reputation of the *Day of Doom* has waned, and few at
the present day know it except by reputation.

The author of this book, whose wand had summoned
up such images of terror, was neither a cynic nor a
misanthrope, though sickness, which generally brings out
these dispositions where they exist, had long been his
doom. His attenuated frame and feeble health were
joined to genial manners; and, though subject to fits of
despondency, he seems generally to have maintained a
cheerful temper, so much so that some of his friends
believed his ills to be imaginary.

Rev. Michael Wigglesworth was born October 28,
1631, probably in Yorkshire, England. He was brought
to this country in 1638, being then seven years old, but
in what ship we are not informed. His father, Edward
Wigglesworth, was one of those resolute Puritans who,
with their families, found an asylum where they could
enjoy their religion without molestation in our then
New England wilderness, the distance of which from
their English homes can hardly be appreciated now.
Here they suffered the severe hardships of a rigorous climate, and the fearful dangers from savage tribes around
them, while uniting to build up villages which are now
cities, and which still retain some of the characteristics
of their Puritan founders. The determined purpose and
strength of principle that conquered every obstacle was
a school of severe training for the children of that
period. It was natural that a father who had endured
so much for conscience' sake should desire to see his
only son a clergyman; and, although the father's means
were not large, the son was devoted to the ministry and
given a thorough education. Michael, after nearly three
years of preparatory studies, entered Harvard College
in 1647. Here he had the good fortune to have for a

tutor the excellent Jonathan Mitchell, "the glory of
the college," and famous as a preacher. The friendship
here begun appears to have continued after both had
left the college walls. Probably the eight stanzas " on
the following work and its author," signed J. Mitchel,
were written by that tutor and preacher, who was a
native of Yorkshire, the county in which Wigglesworth
is believed to have been born.

In 1651 Mr. Wigglesworth graduated, and was soon
after appointed a tutor in the College. Some of his
pupils were men of note in their day. Among them
were, Rev. Shubael Dummer, of York, Me. ; Rev. John
Eliot, of Newton ; and Rev. Samuel Torry, of Wey-
mouth ; but the chief of them, it will be admitted, was
Rev. Increase Mather, D.D., pastor of the second church
in Boston, and for sixteen years president of Harvard
College. That the tutor was faithful to his trust, we
have evidence from the sketch of the funeral sermon
appended to this work, preached by Rev. Cotton Mather,
D.D., son of Increase, who probably derived his infor-
mation from his father.

While a tutor, he prepared himself for the ministry,
and before his father's death he had preached several
times. He was invited, probably in the autumn of
1654, to settle at Malden, as the successor of Rev.
Marmaduke Matthews, but owing to long-continued
sickness was not ordained there till 1656. The precise
date of his ordination is not known, but it must have
been subsequent to August 25, 1656, for his letter of
dismission from the church at Cambridge bears that
date. This letter, addressing the "Church of Christ at
Maldon," states that " the good hand of Divine Provi-
dence hath so disposed that our beloved and highly
esteemed brother, Mr. Wigglesworth, hath his residence
and is employed in the good work of yᵉ Lord amongst

you, and hath cause to desire of us Letters Dismissive
to your church, in order to his joining as a member with
you."

The ill health which had delayed his ordination at
Malden returned soon after his settlement there, and
interrupted his ministry several years. He took a voyage to Bermuda, sailing Sept. 23, 1663, and being absent
about seven months and a half. But the tedious and
stormy voyage seems to have impaired his health so
much that the change of climate afforded him little relief, and he returned much discouraged. He met with
a very cordial welcome from his friends and parish-
ioners.

While he was thus withheld from his ministry, he
employed his time in literary labors. His *Day of Doom*
was published about 1662, the year before his voyage to
Bermuda. The first edition consisting of 1,800 copies,
was sold, with some profit to the author, within a year,
which considering the population and wealth of New
England at that time, shows almost as remarkable a
popularity as that of *Uncle Tom's Cabin.*

While absent on his voyage in search of health, Dec.
9, 1663, Rev. Benjamin Bunker was ordained pastor of
the church at Malden. It seems that a distinction was
observed at this time in New England between pastor
and teacher. Wigglesworth calls Bunker "pastor" in
some verses composed on his death, while on the title-
page of this work he calls himself "teacher." After
Wigglesworth became sole minister, he was probably
considered the pastor. Bunker held this office over six
years, till his death, Feb. 3, 1669-70. In the elegy on
the death of his colleague, Wigglesworth highly extols
Bunker's piety and usefulness. The next colleague of
our author was Rev. Benjamin Blackman, settled about
1674. He supplied the desk four years and upward,

and left in the year 1679. His next colleague was Rev. Thomas Cheever, son of his early teacher, the celebrated New England schoolmaster, Ezekiel Cheever, author of *Latin Accidence*. These three ministers were all educated at Harvard College, Bunker having graduated in 1658, Blackman in 1663, and Cheever in 1677. Mr. Cheever began to preach at Malden Feb. 14, 1679–80, was ordained July 27, 1681, and was dismissed May 20, 1686.

Wigglesworth, though long prevented by sickness from officiating, never resigned his ministerial charge, as appears from a letter which he addressed to Samuel Sprague, July 22, 1687. He was now left alone as minister of the church. He had, however, recovered his health in a measure about this time, which had suffered for nearly twenty years, and for the remainder of his life he continued in public usefulness.

He died on Sunday morning, June 10, 1705, in the 74th year of his age. The epitaph on the last page of this work is believed to have been written by Cotton Mather, as it appears in the appendix to his funeral sermon as by " one that had been gratified by his *Meat out of the Eater* and *Day of Doom.*"

Mr. Wigglesworth had at least three wives: Mary, daughter of Humphrey Reyner, of Rowley; Martha, whose maiden name was probably Mudge; and Sybil, widow of Dr. Jonathan Avery, of Dedham, and daughter of Nathaniel Sparhawk, of Cambridge.

By his first wife he had (1) *Mercy*, b. Feb., 1655–6; m. 1st, [Samuel?] Brackenbury, by whom she had at least one son, William; m. 2d, [Rev. Samuel?] Belcher.

By his second wife, Martha, who d. 11th Sept., 1690, a. 28, he had:—(2) *Abigail*, b. 20th March, 1681; m. Samuel Tappan, 23d Dec., 1700;—(3) *Mary*, b. 21st Sept., 1682; unm. in 1708;—(4) *Martha*, b. 21st Dec., 1683; m. ——— Wheeler;—(5) *Esther*, b. 16th April, 1685; m. 1st, John Sewall, June 8, 1708, who d. 1711; m. 2d, Abraham Tappan, Oct. 21, 1713;—(6) *Dorothy*, b. 22d Feb., 1687–88; m. 2d June, 1709, James Upham;—(7) Rev. *Samuel*, b. 4th Feb., 1689–90, d. 3d Sept,, 1768.

By his third wife, Sybil, who d. 6th Aug., 1708, a. 53, he had:—(8) Prof. *Edward*, D.D., b. about 1692, d. Jan. 16, 1765.

Rev. Samuel Wigglesworth, the elder son, was settled in Hamilton Parish, in Ipswich, Mass., in 1714. He m. 1st, Mary, dau. of John Brintnal, of Winnisimmet, 30th June, 1715, who d. June 6, 1728, a. 28, having borne him four children, Mary, Michael, Martha, and Phebe. He m. March 12, 1730, Martha Brown, and had nine children.

Edward Wigglesworth, D.D., the younger son, took his degree of Bachelor of Arts in 1710, and applied himself to the study of Divinity. He preached for some time in different parishes, and in 1722 was installed Hollis Professor of Divinity of Harvard College. Not long afterward he was chosen one of the fellows of the corporation. He left an only son, who succeeded him as Hollis Professor in the same college, and an only surviving daughter, who married Prof. Sewall.

The following are the various editions of the *Day of Doom*, so far as we have been able to ascertain :

The first edition was published in 1661 or 1662, and the second four years after. These facts are obtained from memoranda by the author, which are printed in the Historical Magazine for December, 1863. An edition was printed in London, England, without the author's name, in 1673. This was, probably, the third impression; the date of the fourth is unknown. The fifth edition is said to have been published in 1701. Mr. Dean has made diligent search and repeated inquiries, but can only find two or three copies of the edition of 1673, and several fragments which must have been parts of some of the other editions.

There was an edition published at Newcastle, in England, in 1711. The next edition was published in 1715, called "the 6th edition, enlarged, with Scripture and marginal notes"—"printed by John Allen, for Benjamin Eliot, at his shop in King street." From this edition, which was evidently the seventh, the present one is reprinted, being carefully compared with that of 1673. Another edition appeared in 1751, "Printed and sold by Thomas Fleet, at the Heart and Crown, in Cornhill,"

Boston. The next edition appeared in 1811, "Published by E. Little & Company, Newburyport," Mass. The last edition, prior to the present, was published in Boston in 1828, by Charles Ewer.

Besides the *Day of Doom*, Mr. Wigglesworth published, in 1669, "Meat out of the Eater ; or, Meditations concerning the necessity and usefulness of Afflictions unto God's Children." The "fourth edition" appeared in 1689, and subsequent editions in 1717 and 1770. In 1686 he preached an Election Sermon, which was printed by the colony. Among his unpublished writings is a poem entitled "God's Controversy with New England, written in the time of the great Drought, Anno 1662. By a lover of New England's prosperity."

Mr. Wigglesworth borrowed little from other poets, and what he borrowed was probably from the commentaries and theological treatises with which his library abounded, rather than from the poets. Not that his style is wholly prosaic, for there are passages in his writings that are truly poetical, both in thought and expression, and which show that he was capable of attaining a higher position as a poet than can now be claimed for him. The roughness of his verses was surely not owing to carelessness or indolence, for neither of them was characteristic of the man. The true explanation may be, that he sacrificed his poetical taste to his theology, and that, for the sake of inculcating sound doctrine, he was willing to write in halting numbers.

The author of the *Day of Doom*, belonging to the straitest sect of Puritans, was, like many others of that sect, a man of generous feeling toward his fellows. Rev. Dr. Peabody calls him "a man of the beatitudes." Obedience to the supreme law gave a heavenly lustre to his example and a sweet fragrance to his memory. The clergy of his day possessed a deep religious earnestness and a fervent piety. They were Bible students and men of prayer. Even many who consider them erroneous in doctrine, are willing to allow that they were strict in morals; that, if they were wrong in faith, they were right in life ; that, if their creed was opaque, their hearts were luminous; and that, if their vision did not discern the additional light which the saintly Robinson had prophesied was yet to break forth from God's Word, they sincerely accepted the light they saw. They were patient, hopeful, humble, believing, faithful. They stood on a higher plane than their successors, and exercised a proportionally higher power over their hearers. Their people revered them, were constant in attendance on their services, and submitted gladly to their sway.

AUTOBIOGRAPHY.

I was born of Godly Parents, that feared ye Lord greatly, even from their youth, but in an ungodly Place, where ye generality of ye people rather derided than imitated their piety; in a place where, to my knowledge, their children had Learnt wickedness betimes; in a place that was consumed with fire in a great part of it, after God had brought them out of it. These godly parents of mine meeting with opposition and persecution for Religion, because they went from their own Parish church to hear ye word and Receiv ye Lords supper &c, took up resolutions to pluck up their stakes and remove themselves to New England : and accordingly they did so, Leaving dear Relations, friends and acquaintance, their native Land, a new built house, a flourishing Trade, to expose themselves to ye hazzard of ye seas, and to ye Distressing difficulties of a howling wilderness, that they might enjoy Liberty of Conscience and Christ in his ordinances. And the Lord brought them hither and Landed them at Charlstown, after many difficulties and hazzards, and me along with them, being then a child not full seven years old. After about 7 weeks stay at Charlstown, my parents removed again by sea to New Haven in ye month of October. In our passage thither we were in great Danger by a storm which drove us upon a Beach of sand where we lay beating til another Tide fetcht us off; but God carried us to our port in safety. Winter approaching we dwelt in a cellar partly under ground covered with earth the first winter. But I remember that one great rain, brake in upon us and drencht me so in my bed, being asleep, that I fell sick upon it; but yᵉ Lord in mercy spar'd my life and restored my health. When yᵉ next summer was come I was sent to school to Mr. Ezekiel Cheever, who at that time taught school in his own house, and under him in a year or two I profited so much through yᵉ blessing of God, that I began to make Latin and to get forward apace. But God who is infinitely wise and absolutely soverain, and gives no account concerning any of his proceedings, was pleased about this time to visit my father with Lameness which grew upon him more and more to his dying Day, though he liv'd under it 13 years. He wanting help was fain to take me off from school to follow other employments for yᵉ space of 3 or 4 years, until I had lost all that I had gained in the Latin Tongue. But when I was now in my fourteenth year, my Father, who I suppose was not wel satisfied in keeping me from Learning whereto I had been designed from my infancy, and not judging me fit for husbandry, sent me to school again, though at that time I had little or no disposition to it, but I was willing to submit to his authority therein and accordingly I went to school under no small disadvantage and discouragement, seing those that were far inferior to me, by my discontinuance now gotten far before me. But in a little time it appeared to be of God, who was pleased to facilitate my work and bless my studies that I soon recovered what I had lost, and gained a great deal more, so that in 2 years and 3 quarters I was judged fit for yᵉ Colledge and thither I was sent far from my parents and acquaintance among strangers. But when father and mother both forsook me then yᵉ Lord took care of me. It was an act of great self denial in my father that notwithstanding his own lameness and great weakness of Body which required yᵉ service and helpfulness of a son, and having but one son to be yᵉ staff of his age and supporter of his weakness, he would yet for my good, be content to deny himself of that comfort and Assistance I might have Lent him. It was also an evident proof of a strong Faith in him, in that he durst adventure to send me to yᵉ Colledge, though his estate was but small and little enough to maintain himself and small family left at home. And God let him Live to see how acceptable to himself this service was in giving up his only son to yᵉ Lord and bringing him up to Learning; especially yᵉ Lively actings of his faith and self denial herein. For first, notwithstanding his great weakness of body, yet he Lived til I was so far brought up as that I was called to be a fellow of yᵉ Colledge and improved in Publick service there, and until I had preached several Times; yea and more than so, he Lived to see and hear what God had done for my soul in turning me from Darkness to light and from yᵉ power of Sathan unto God, which filled his heart full of joy and thankfulness beyond what can be expressed. And for his outward estate, that was so far from being sunk by what he spent from year to year upon my education, that in 6 years time it was plainly doubled, which himself took great notice of, and spake of it to myself and others, to ye praise of God, with Admiration and thankfulness. And after he had lived under great and sore affliction for ye space of 13 years a pattern of faith, patience, humility, and heavenly mindedness, having done his work in my education and receiv'd an answer to his prayers, God took him to his Heavenly Rest, where he is now reaping ye fruits of his Labors. When I came first to ye Colledge, I had indeed enjoyed ye benefit of Religious and strict education, and God in his mercy and pitty kept me from scandalous sins before I came thither and after I came there, but alas I had a naughty vile heart and was acted by corrupt nature, therefore could propound no Right and noble ends, but acted from self and for self. I was indeed studious and strove to outdoe my compeers, but it was for honour and applause and preferment and such poor Beggarly ends. Thus I had my Ends and God had his Ends far differing from mine, yet it pleased him to Bless my studies, and to make me grow in Knowledge both in ye tongues and inferior Arts and also in Divinity. But when I had been there about three years and a half; God in his Love and Pitty to my soul wrought a great change in me, both in heart and Life, and from that time forward I learnt to study with God and for God. And whereas before that, I had thoughts of applying myself to ye study and Practice of Physick, I wholy laid aside those thoughts, and did chuse to serve Christ in ye work of ye ministry if he would please to fit me for it and to accept of my service in that great work.

NOTE.—In the foregoing Autobiography the original spelling is retained. In the following poems the spelling is modernized. The use of the acute accent (´) to indicate the former pronunciation of the final *ed* as a separate syllable will be obvious; in other exceptional cases the old apostrophe is retained. In a few instances the termination *tion* is divided by a hyphen, to indicate its pronunciation as two syllables (*she-on*). The modern double commas are also used to mark quotations.

W. H. B.

TO THE CHRISTIAN READER.

READER, I am a fool,
And have adventuréd
To play the fool this once for Christ,
The more his fame to spread.
If this my foolishness
Help thee to be more wise, ·
I have attainéd what I seek,
And what I only prize.

Thou wonderest, perhaps,
That I in Print appear,
Who to the Pulpit dwell so nigh,
Yet come so seldom there.
The God of Heaven knows
What grief to me it is,
To be withheld from serving Christ;
No sorrow like to this.

This is the sorest pain
That I have felt or feel ;
Yet have I stood some shocks that might
Make stronger men to reel.
I find more true delight
In serving of the Lord,
Than all the good things upon Earth,
Without it, can afford.

And could my strength endure
That work I count so dear,
Not all the Riches of Peru
Should hire me to forbear.
But I'm a Prisoner,
Under a heavy Chain;
Almighty God's afflicting hand
Doth me by force restrain.

Yet some (*I know*) do judge
Mine inability
To come abroad and do Christ's work,
To be Melancholly;
And that I'm not so weak
As I myself conceit:
But who in other things have found
Me so conceited yet?

Or who of all my Friends
That have my trials seen,
Can tell the time in sevén years
When I have dumpish been?
Some think my voice is strong,
Most times when I do Preach;
But ten days after, what I feel
And suffer few can reach.

My prison'd thoughts break forth,
When open'd is the door,
With greater force and violence,
And strain my voice the more.
But vainly do they tell
That I am growing stronger,
Who hear me speak in half an hour,
Till I can speak no longer.

Some for because they see not
My cheerfulness to fail,
Nor that I am disconsolate,
Do think I nothing ail.
If they had borne my griefs,
Their courage might have fail'd them,
And all the Town (perhaps) have known
(Once and again) what ail'd them.

But why should I complain
That have so good a God,
That doth mine heart with comfort fill
Ev'n whilst I feel his Rod ?
In God I have been strong,
But wearied and worn out,
And joy'd in him, when twenty woes
Assail'd me round about.

Nor speak I this to boast,
But make Apology
For mine own self, and answer those
That fail in Charity.
I am, alas ! as frail,
Impatient a creature,
As most that tread upon the ground,
And have as bad a nature.

Let God be magnified,
Whose everlasting strength
Upholds me under sufferings
Of more than ten years' length ;
Through whose Almighty pow'r
Although I am surrounded
With sorrows more than can be told,
Yet am I not confounded.

For his dear sake have I
This service undertaken,
For I am bound to honor him
Who hath not me forsaken.
I am a Debtor too,
Unto the sons of Men,
Whom, wanting other means, I would
Advantage with my Pen.

I would, but ah! my strength,
When triéd, proves so small,
That to the ground without effect
My wishes often fall.
Weak heads, and hands, and states,
Great things cannot produce ;
And therefore I this little Piece
Have publish'd for thine use.

Although the thing be small,
Yet my good will therein,
Is nothing less than if it had
A larger Volume been.
Accept it then in love,
And read it for thy good ;
There's nothing in 't can do thee hurt,
If rightly understood.

The God of Heaven grant
These Lines so well to speed,
That thou the things of thine own peace
Through them may'st better heed ;
And may'st be stirréd up
To stand upon thy guard,
That Death and Judgment may not come
And find thee unprepar'd.

Oh get a part in Christ,
And make the Judge thy Friend;
So shalt thou be assuréd of
A happy, glorious end.
Thus prays thy real Friend
And Servant for Christ's sake,
Who, had he strength, would not refuse
More pains for thee to take.

MICHAEL WIGGLESWORTH.

ON THE FOLLOWING WORK AND ITS AUTHOR.

A VERSE may find him who a sermon flies,
Saith Herbert well.   Great truths to dress in Meter.
Becomes a Preacher, who men's Souls doth prize,
That Truth in Sugar roll'd may taste the sweeter.
   No cost too great, no care too curious is
    To set forth Truth and win men's Souls to bliss.

In costly Verse, and most laborious Rhymes,
Are dish'd up here Truths worthy most regard:
No Toys, nor Fables (Poets' wonted crimes)
Here be, but things of worth, with wit prepar'd.
   Reader, fall to, and if thy taste be good,
    Thou'lt praise the Cook, and say, 'Tis choicest Food.

David's affliction bred us many a Psalm,
From Caves, from mouth of Graves that Singer sweet
Oft tun'd his Soul-felt notes: for not in 's calm,
But storms, to write most Psalms God made him meet.
   Affliction turn'd his Pen to Poetry,
    Whose serious strains do here before thee lie.

This man with many griefs afflicted sore,
Shut up from speaking much in sickly Cave,
Thence painful seizure hath to write the more,

And send thee Counsels from the mouth o' th' Grave.
One foot i' th' other world long time hath been,
Read, and thou'lt say, His heart is all therein.

Oh, happy Cave, that's to mount Nebo turn'd !
Oh, happy prisoner that's at liberty
To walk through th' other World! the Bonds are burn'd,
(But nothing else) in Furnace fiéry.
　　Such fires unfetter Saints, and set more free
　　Their unscorch'd Souls for Christ's sweet company.

Cheer on, sweet Soul, although in briny tears
Steept is thy seed ; though dying every day ;
Thy sheaves shall joyful be when Christ appears,
To change our death and pain to life for aye.
　　The weepers now shall laugh ; the jovial laughter
　　Of vain ones here shall turn to tears hereafter.

Judge right, and his restraint is our Reproof.
The Sins of Hearers Preachers' Lips do close,
And make their Tongue to cleave unto its roof,
Which else would check and cheer full freely those
　　That need.　But from this Eater comes some Meat,
　　And sweetness good from this affliction great.

In those vast Woods a Christian Poet sings
(Where whilom Heathen wild were only found)
Of things to come, the last and greatest things
Which in our Ears aloud should ever sound.
　　Of Judgment dread, Hell, Heaven, Eternity,
　　Reader, think oft, and help thy thoughts thereby.

J. MITCHEL.

A PRAYER

CHRIST THE JUDGE OF THE WORLD.

O Dearest, Dread, most glorious King !
I'll of thy justest Judgments sing :
Do thou my head and heart inspire,
To Sing aright, as I desire.
Thee, thee alone I'll invocate,
For I do much abominate
To call the Muses to mine aid :
Which is th' Unchristian use and trade
Of some that Christians would be thought,
And yet they worship worse than naught.
Oh ! what a deal of Blasphemy,
And Heathenish Impiety,
In Christian Poets may be found,
Where Heathen gods with praise are crown'd !
They make Jehovah to stand by
Till Juno, Venus, Mercury,
With frowning Mars, and thund'ring Jove,
Rule Earth below, and Heav'n above.
But I have learn'd to pray to none,
Save unto God in Christ alone.
Nor will I laud, no, not in jest,
That which I know God doth detest.
I reckon it a damning evil,
To give God's Praises to the Devil.
Thou, Christ, art he to whom I pray ;
Thy Glory fain I would display.
Oh ! guide me by thy sacred Sprite,
So to indite, and so to write,
That I thine holy Name may praise,
And teach the Sons of Men thy ways.

THE

DAY OF DOOM.

I.

STILL was the night, serene and bright,
   when all Men sleeping lay;
Calm was the season, and carnal reason
   thought so 'twould last for aye.
"Soul, take thine ease, let sorrow cease;
   much good thou hast in store:"
This was their Song, their Cups among,
   the evening before.

The security
of the World
before Christ's
coming to judg-
ment.
Luke 12 : 19.

II.

Wallowing in all kind of Sin,
   vile Wretches lay secure;
The best of men had scarcely then
   their Lamps kept in good ure.
Virgins unwise, who through disguise
   amongst the best were number'd,
Had clos'd their eyes; yea, and the Wise
   through sloth and frailty slumber'd.

Mat. 25 : 5.

III.

Like as of old, when men grew bold,
   God's threat'nings to contemn,
Who stopt their Ear, and would not hear
Mat. 24: 37, 38.   when Mercy warnéd them,
   But took their course, without remorse,
      till God began to pour
   Destructi-on the World upon,
      in a tempestuous show'r;

IV.

1 Thes. 5 : 3.   Who put away the evil day,
      and drown'd their cares and fears,
   Till drown'd were they, and swept away
      by vengeance unawares;
   So at the last, whilst men sleep fast
      in their security,
   Surpris'd they are in such a snare
      As cometh suddenly.

V.

The sudden- For at midnight breaks forth a light,
ness, Majesty,   which turns the night to day,
and Terror of
Christ's appear- And speedily an hideous cry
ing.   doth all the World dismay.
Mat. 25: 6.
2 Pet. 3 : 10. Sinners awake, their hearts do ache,
      trembling their loins surpriseth;
   Amaz'd with fear, by what they hear,
      each one of them ariseth.

VI.

They rush from beds with giddy heads,
   and to their windows run,
Viewing this light, which shines more bright
   than doth the noon-day Sun.

Straightway appears (they see't with tears)
　the Son of God most dread,
Who with his Train comes on amain   Mat. 24 :
　to judge both Quick and Dead.   29, 30.

VII.

Before his face the Heav'ns give place,
　and Skies are rent asunder,
With mighty voice and hideous noise,
　more terrible than Thunder.
His Brightness damps Heav'n's glorious Lamps
　and makes them hide their heads ;
As if afraid and quite dismay'd,   2 Pet. 8 : 10.
　they quit their wonted steads.

VIII.

Ye sons of men that durst contemn
　the Threat'nings of God's Word,
How cheer you now ? Your hearts, I trow,
　are thrill'd as with a sword.
Now Atheist blind, whose brutish mind
　a God could never see,
Dost thou perceive, dost now believe
　that Christ thy Judge shall be ?

IX.

Stout Courages, (whose hardiness
　could Death and Hell outface,)
Are you as bold, now you behold
　your Judge draw near apace ?
They cry, "No, no, Alas ! and woe !
　our courage all is gone :
Our hardiness (fool hardiness)
　hath us undone, undone!"

X.

Rev. 6 : 15.   No heart so bold, but now grows cold,
                    and almost dead with fear;
                 No eye so dry but now can cry,
                    and pour out many a tear.
                 Earth's Potentates and pow'rful States,
                    Captains and Men of Might,
                 Are quite abasht, their courage dasht,
                    at this most dreadful sight.

XI.

Mat. 24 : 30.   Mean men lament, great men do rent
                    their Robes, and tear their hair;
                 They do not spare their flesh to tear
                    through horrible despair.
                 All kindreds wail; all hearts do fail;
                    Horror the World doth fill
                 With weeping eyes and loud out-cries,
                    yet knows not how to kill.

XII.

Rev. 6 : 15, 16. Some hide themselves in Caves and Delves,
                    in places under ground:
                 Some rashly leap into the Deep,
                    to 'scape by being drown'd:
                 Some to the Rocks (O senseless blocks!)
                    and woody Mountains run,
                 That there they might this fearful sight,
                    and dreaded Presence shun.

XIII.

                 In vain do they to Mountains say,
                    "Fall on us and us hide
                 From Judge's ire, more hot than Fire,
                    for who may it abide?"

No hiding place can from his Face
    sinners at all conceal,
Whose flaming Eye hid things doth spy,
    and darkest things reveal.

XIV.

The Judge draws nigh, exalted high   Mat. 25 : 21.
    upon a lofty Throne,
Amidst the throng of Angels strong,
    lo, Israel's Holy One !
The excellence of whose Presence
    and awful Majesty,
Amazeth Nature, and every Creature
    doth more than terrify.

XV.

The Mountains smoke, the Hills are shook,   Rev. 6 : 14.
    the Earth is rent and torn,
As if she should be clear dissolv'd
    or from her center borne.
The Sea doth roar, forsakes the shore,
    and shrinks away for fear ;
The wild beasts flee into the sea,
    so soon as he draws near,

XVI.

Whose Glory bright, whose wond'rous Might,
    whose Power Imperial,
So far surpass whatever was
    in Realms Terrestrial,
That tongues of men (nor Angel's pen)
    Cannot the same express ;
And therefore I must pass it by,
    lest speaking should transgress.   Thes. 4 : 16.

2

XVII.

Resurrection
of the Dead.
John 5 : 28, 29.

Before his Throne a Trump is blown,
    proclaiming th' Day of Doom ;
Forthwith he cries, " *Ye Dead arise*
    and unto Judgment come."
No sooner said, but 'tis obey'd ;
    Sepulchers open'd are ;
Dead bodies all rise at his call,
    and's mighty Power declare.

XVIII.

Both Sea and Land at his command,
    their Dead at once surrender ;
The Fire and Air constrainéd are
    also their dead to tender.
The mighty Word of this great Lord
    links Body and Soul together,
Both of the Just and the unjust,
    to part no more for ever.

XIX.

The living
changed.
Luke 20 : 36.
1 Cor. 15 : 52.

The same translates from Mortal states
    to Immortality,
All that survive and be alive,
    in th' twinkling of an eye ;
That so they may abide for aye,
    to endless weal or woe :
Both the Renate and Reprobate
    are made to die no moe.

XX.

All brought
to Judgment.
Mat. 24 : 31.

His wingéd Hosts fly through all coasts,
    together gathering
Both good and bad, both Quick and Dead,
    and all to Judgment bring.

Out of their holes those creeping Moles,
   that hid themselves for fear,
By force they take, and quickly make
   before the Judge appear.

XXI.

Thus every one before the Throne
   of Christ the Judge is brought,
Both righteous and impious,
   that good or ill hath wrought.
A separation and diff'ring station
   by Christ appointed is
(To sinners sad) 'twixt good and bad,
   'twixt Heirs of woe and bliss.

2 Cor. 5 : 10.
The Sheep
separated
from the Goats.
Mat. 25 : 32.

XXII.

At Christ's right hand the Sheep do stand,
   his holy Martyrs, who
For his dear Name suffering shame,
   calamity and woe,
Like Champions stood and with their Blood
   their Testimony sealéd ;
Whose innocence without offence
   ·to Christ their Judge appealéd.

Who are
Christ's
Sheep.
Mat. 5 : 10, 11.

XXIII.

Next unto whom there find a room
   all Christ's afflicted ones,
Who being chastis'd, neither despis'd
   nor sank amidst their groans ;
Who by the Rod were turn'd to God,
   and lovéd him the more,
Not murmuring nor quarrelling
   when they were chast'ned sore.

Heb. 12 : 5,
6, 7.

XXIV.

Moreover, such as lovéd much,
    that had not such a trial,
As might constrain to so great pain,
Luke 7 : 41, 47.   and such deep self-denial,
Yet ready were the Cross to bear,
    when Christ them call'd thereto,
And did rejoice to hear his voice,—
    they're counted Sheep also.

XXV.

Christ's flock of Lambs there also stands,
John 21 : 15.   whose Faith was weak, yet true,
Mat. 19 : 14.
John 3 : 3.   All sound Believers (Gospel receivers)
    whose Grace was small, but grew ;
And them among an Infant throng
    of Babes, for whom Christ died ;
Whom for his own, by ways unknown
    to Men, he sanctified.

XXVI.

All stand before their Savi-or,
    in long white Robes yclad,
Rev. 6 : 11.   Their countenance full of pleasance,
Phil. 3 : 21.   appearing wond'rous glad.
O glorious sight !   Behold how bright
    dust-heaps are made to shine,
Conforméd so their Lord unto,
    whose Glory is Divine.

XXVII.

The Goats   At Christ's left hand the Goats do stand,
described, or   all whining Hypocrites
the several
sorts of Repro- Who for self-ends did seem Christ's friends,
bates on the   but foster'd guileful sprites ;

Who Sheep resembled, but they dissembled,   left hand.
   (their hearts were not sincere,)   Mat. 24 : 51.
Who once did throng Christ's Lambs among,
   but now must not come near.

XXVIII.

Apostates base and run-aways,   Luke 11 : 24,
   such as have Christ forsaken,   26.
                                    Heb. 6 : 4, 5, 6.
Of whom the Devil, with seven more evil,   Heb. 10 : 29.
   hath fresh possession taken ;
Sinners ingrain, reserv'd to pain,
   and torments most severe,
Because 'gainst light they sinn'd with spite,
   are also placéd there.

XXIX.

There also stand a num'rous band,
   that no profession made
Of Godliness, nor to redress   Luke 12 : 47.
   their ways at all essay'd ;   Prov. 1 : 24, 26.
                                   Job 8 : 19.
Who better knew, but (sinful Crew)
   Gospel and Law despiséd,
Who all Christ's knocks withstood like blocks,
   and would not be advised.

XXX.

Moreover, there with them appear
   a number, numberless,   Gal. 3 : 10.
Of great and small, vile wretches all,   1 Cor. 6 : 9.
   that did God's Law transgress ;   Rev. 21 : 8.
Idolaters, false worshippers,
   Profaners of God's Name,
Who not at all thereon did call,
   or took in vain the same.

XXXI.

Exod. 20 : 7, 8. Blasphemers lewd, and Swearers shrewd,
      scoffers at Purity,
    That hated God, contemn'd his Rod,
      and lov'd Security;
2 Thes. 1 : 6, Sabbath-polluters, Saints-persecutors,
8, 9.   presumptuous men and proud,
    Who never lov'd those that reprov'd;
      all stand amongst this crowd.

XXXII.

    Adulterers and Whoremongers
Heb. 13 : 4.   were there, with all unchast;
1 Cor. 6 : 10. There Covetous and Ravenous,
      that riches got too fast:
    Who us'd vile ways themselves to raise
      t' Estates and worldly wealth,
    Oppression by or knavery,
      by force, or fraud, or stealth.

XXXIII.

    Moreover, there together were
      children flagiti-ous,
    And Parents who did them undo
Zach. 5 : 3, 4.   by nurture vici-ous.
Gal. 5 : 19, False-witness-bearers and self-forswearers,
20, 21.   Murd'rers and Men of Blood,
    Witches, Enchanters, and Ale-house haunters,
      beyond account there stood.

XXXIV.

    Their place there find all Heathen blind
      that Nature's light abus'd,
Rom. 2 : 13. Although they had no tidings glad
      of Gospel grace refus'd

There stand all Nations and Generations
   of Adam's Progeny,   [not,
Whom Christ redeem'd not, whom he esteem'd
   through Infidelity;

XXXV.

Who no Peace-maker, no undertaker,
   to shroud them from God's ire,
Ever obtain'd; they must be pain'd   Acts 4 : 12.
   with everlasting fire.
These num'rous bands, wringing their hands,
   and weeping all stand there,
Filléd with anguish, whose hearts do languish,
   through self-tormenting fear.

XXXVI.

Fast by them stand at Christ's left hand,
   the Lion fierce and fell,
The Dragon bold, that Serpent old,
   that hurried Souls to Hell.   1 Cor. 6 : 3.
There also stand, under command,
   legions of Sprites unclean,
And hellish Fiends, that are no friends
   to God, nor unto Men.

XXXVII.

With dismal chains, and strongest reins,
   like Prisoners of Hell,   Jude 6.
They're held in place before Christ's face,
   till He their Doom shall tell.
These void of tears, but fill'd with fears,
   and dreadful expectation
Of endless pains and scalding flames,
   stand waiting for Damnation.

XXXVIII.

All silence keep both Goats and Sheep
    before the Judge's Throne;
With mild aspect to his Elect
    then speaks the Holy One:
" My Sheep draw near, your Sentence hear,
    which is to you no dread,
Who clearly now discern and know
    your sins are pardonéd.

The Saints
cleared and
justified.

XXXIX.

" 'Twas meet that ye should judgéd be,
    that so the World may spy
No cause of grudge, when as I judge
    and deal impartially.
Know therefore all both great and small,
    the ground and reason why
These Men do stand at my right hand
    and look so cheerfully.

2 Cor. 5 : 10.
Eccl. 3 : 17.
John 3 : 18.

XL.

" These Men be those my Father chose
    before the World's foundation,
And to me gave, that I should save
    from Death and Condemnation ;
For whose dear sake I flesh did take,
    was of a Woman born,
And did inure myself t' endure
    unjust reproach and scorn.

Job 17 : 6.
Eph. 1 : 4.

XLI.

" For then it was that I did pass
    through sorrows many a one ;
That I drank up that bitter Cup
    which made me sigh and groan.

The Cross's pain I did sustain ;
  yea more, my Father's ire
I underwent, my Blood I spent
  to save them from Hell-fire.

Rev. 1 : 5.

XLII.

" Thus I esteeméd, thus I redceméd
  all those from every Nation,
That they may be (as now you see)
  a chosen Generation.
What if ere while they were as vile
  and bad as any be,
And yet from all their guilt and thrall
  at once I set them free ?

Eph. 2 : 1, 3.

XLIII.

" My grace to one is wrong to none ;
  none can Election claim ;
Amongst all those their souls that lose,
  none can Rejection blame.
He that may choose, or else refuse,
  all men to save or spill,
May this Man choose, and that refuse,
  redeeming whom he will.

Mat. 23 : 13,
15.
Rom. 9 : 20, 21.

XLIV.

" But as for those whom I have chose
  Salvation's heirs to be,
I underwent their punishment,
  and therefore set them free.
I bore their grief, and their relief
  by suffering procur'd,
That they of bliss and happiness
  might firmly be assur'd.

Isa. 53 : 4,
5, 11.

XLV.

"And this my grace they did embrace,
   believing on my Name ;
Which Faith was true, the fruits do shew
   proceeding from the same ;—
Their Penitence, their Pati-ence,
   their Love and Self-denial,
In suff'ring losses and bearing Crosses,
   when put upon the trial ;—

Acts 1 : 3, 48.
Jam. 2 : 18.
Heb. 12 : 7.
Mat. 19 : 29.

XLVI.

"Their sin forsaking, their cheerful taking
   my Yoke, their Charity
Unto the Saints in all their wants,
   and in them unto me ;—
These things do clear, and make appear
   their Faith to be unfeignéd,
And that a part in my desert
   and purchase they have gainéd.

1 John 3 : 3.
Mat. 25 : 39, 40.

XLVII.

"Their debts are paid, their peace is made,
   their sins remitted are ;
Therefore at once I do pronounce,
   and openly declare,
That Heav'n is theirs, that they be Heirs
   of Life and of Salvation ;
Nor ever shall they come at all
   to Death or to Damnation.

Isa. 53 : 11, 12.
Rom. 8 : 16,
17, 33, 34.
John 3 : 18.

XLVIII.

"Come blessed Ones and sit on Thrones,
   judging the World with me ;
Come and possess your happiness,
   and bought felicity ;

Luke 22 : 29, 30.

Henceforth no fears, no care, no tears,
   no sin shall you annoy,
Nor any thing that grief doth bring :
   Eternal Rest enjoy.

Mat. 19 : 28.

XLIX.

" You bore the Cross, you suffer'd loss
   of all for my Name's sake ;
Receive the Crown that's now your own ;
   come, and a Kingdom take."
Thus spake the Judge : the wicked grudge
   and grind their teeth in vain ;
They see with groans these plac'd on Thrones,
   which addeth to their pain :

Mat. 25 : 34.
They are
placed on
Thrones to join
with Christ in
judging the
wicked.

L.

That those whom they did wrong and slay,
   must now their Judgment see !
Such whom they slighted and once despited,
   must now their Judges be !
Thus 'tis decreed, such is their meed,
   and guerdon glorious ;
With Christ they sit, judging it fit
   to plague the Impious.

Cor. 6 : 2.

LI.

The wicked are brought to the Bar.
   like guilty Malefactors,
That oftentimes of bloody Crimes
   and Treasons have been Actors.
Of wicked Men, none are so mean
   as there to be neglected ;
Nor none so high in dignity
   as there to be respected.

The wicked
brought to
the Bar.
Rom. 2 : 3, 6,
11.

LII.

The glorious Judge will privilege
  nor Emperor nor King;
But every one that hath misdone
Rev. 6 : 15, 16.   doth unto judgment bring.
Isa. 30 : 33.
And every one that hath misdone,
  the Judge impartially
Condemneth to eternal woe,
  and endless misery.

LIII.

Thus one and all, thus great and small,
  the Rich as well as Poor,
And those of place, as the most base,
  do stand the Judge before.
They are arraign'd, and there detain'd
  before Christ's Judgment seat,
With trembling fear their Doom to hear,
  and feel his Anger's heat.

LIV.

There Christ demands at all their hands
  a strict and straight account
Of all things done under the Sun,
Eccl. 11 : 9,   whose number far surmount
12, 14.
Man's wit and thought: they all are brought
  unto this solemn Trial,
And each offense with evidence,
  so that there's no denial.

LV.

There's no excuse for their abuse,
  since their own Consciences
More proof give in of each Man's sin,
  than thousand Witnesses.

Though formerly this faculty
  had grossly been abuséd,
(Men could it stifle, or with it trifle,
  when as it them accuséd,)

LVI.

Now it comes in, and every sin
  unto Men's charge doth lay ;
It judgeth them and doth condemn,
  though all the World say nay.
It so stingeth and tortureth,
  it worketh such distress,
That each Man's self against himself,
  is forcéd to confess.

LVII.

It's vain, moreover, for Men to cover
  the least Iniquity ;
The Judge hath seen, and privy been
  to all their villainy.
He unto light and open sight
  the work of darkness brings ;
He doth unfold both new old,
  both known and hidden things.

Secret sins and
works of dark-
ness brought to
light.
Ps. 139 : 2, 4,
12.
Rom. 2 : 16.

LVIII.

All filthy facts and secret acts,
  however closely done,
And long conceal'd, are there reveal'd
  before the mid-day Sun.
Deeds of the night, shunning the light,
  which darkest corners sought,
To fearful blame, and endless shame,
  are there most justly brought.

Eccl. 12 : 14.

LIX.

And as all facts, and grosser acts,
    so every word and thought,
Erroneous notion and lustful motion,
    are unto Judgment brought.
No Sin so small and trivial,
    but hither it must come;
Nor so long past but now at last
    it must receive a doom.

Mat. 12 : 36.
Rom. 7 : 7.

LX.

At this sad season, Christ asks a Reason
    (with just austerity)
Of Grace refus'd, of light abus'd
    so oft, so wilfully;
Of Talents lent, by them misspent
    and on their Lust bestown,
Which if improv'd as it behoov'd
    Heav'n might have been their own;

An account
demanded of all
their actions.
John 5 : 40, and
3 : 19.
Mat. 25 : 19, 27.

LXI.

Of times neglected, of means rejected,
    of God's long-suffering
And Pati-ence, to Penitence
    that sought hard hearts to bring;
Why chords of love did nothing move,
    to shame or to remorse?
Why warnings grave, and counsels, have
    naught chang'd their sinful course?

Rom. 2 : 4, 5.

LXII.

Why chastenings, and evils things,
    why judgments so severe,
Prevailéd not with them a jot,
    nor wrought an awful fear?

Isa. 1 : 5.

Why promises of Holiness,
  and new Obedience,   Jer. 2 : 20.
They oft did make, but always brake
  the same, to God's offense ?

LXIII.

Why still Hell-ward, without regard,
  they bold venturéd,   John 3 : 19, etc.
And chose Damnation before Salvation,   Prov. 8 : 36.
  when it was offeréd?   Luke 12 : 20, 21.
Why sinful pleasures and earthly treasures,
  like fools, they prizéd more
Than Heav'nly wealth, Eternal health,
  and all Christ's Royal store ?

LXIV.

Why, when he stood off'ring his Blood
  to wash them from their sin,   Luke 13 : 34.
They would embrace no saving Grace,   John 5 : 40, and
  but liv'd and died therein?   15 22.
Such aggravations, where no evasions,
  nor false pretences hold,
Exaggerate and cumulate
  guilt more than can be told.

LXV.

They multiply and magnify
  Men's gross Iniquities ;
They draw down wrath (as Scripture saith)
  out of God's treasuries.
Thus all their ways Christ open lays
  to Men and Angels' view,
And as they were makes them appear
  in their own proper hue.

LXVI.

Thus he doth find of all Mankind,

Rom. 3 : 10, 12. that stand at his left hand,

No mother's son but hath misdone,
and broken God's command.
All have transgress'd, even the best,
and merited God's wrath,
Unto their own perditi-on
and everlasting scath.

LXVII.

Earth's dwellers all, both great and small,

Rom. 6 : 23. have wrought iniquity,

And suffer must (for it is just)
Eternal misery.
Amongst the many there come not any,
before the Judge's face,
That able are themselves to clear,
of all this cursed Race.

LXVIII.

Nevertheless, they all express,

Hypocrites plead for them-selves. (Christ granting liberty,)

What for their way they have to say,
how they have liv'd, and why.
They all draw near and seek to clear
themselves by making pleas;
There Hypocrites, false-hearted wights,
do make such pleas as these :

LXIX.

" Lord, in thy Name, and by the same,

Mat. 7 : 21, 22, 23. we Devils dispossess'd;

We rais'd the dead and minist'red
Succor to the distress'd.

Our painful teaching and pow'rful preaching
  by thine own wondrous might,
Did throughly win to God from sin
  many a wretched wight."

LXX.

" All this," quoth he, " may granted be,
  and your case little better'd,
Who still remain under a chain
  and many irons fetter'd.
You that the dead have quickenéd,
  and rescu'd from the grave,
Yourselves were dead, yet ne'er needéd
  a Christ your souls to save.

The Judge replyeth.
John 6 : 70.
1 Cor. 9 : 27.

LXXI.

" You that could preach, and others teach
  what way to life doth lead,
Why were you slack to find that track
  and in that way to tread ?
How could you bear to see or hear
  of others freed at last
From Satan's paws, whilst in his jaws
  yourselves were held more fast ?

Rom. 2 : 19, 21,
22, 23.

LXXII.

" Who though you knew Repentance true,
  and Faith is my great Name,
The only mean to quit you clean,
  from punishment and blame,
Yet took no pain true Faith to gain,
  such as might not deceive,
Nor would repent with true intent,
  your evil deeds to leave.

John 9 : 41.
Rev. 2 : 21, 22.

LXXIII.

"His Master's will how to fulfil
the servant that well knew,
Yet left undone his duty known,
more plagues to him are due.
You against light perverted right;
wherefore it shall be now
For Sidon and for Sodom's Land
more easy than for you."

Luke 12 : 47.
Mat. 11 : 21,
22, 24.

LXXIV.

"But we have in thy presence been,"
say some, "and eaten there.
Did we not eat thy Flesh for meat,
and feed on Heav'nly Cheer ?
Whereon who feed shall never need,
as thou thyself dost say,
Nor shall they die eternally,
but live with Christ for aye.

Another plea of
the Hypocrites.
Luke 13 : 20.

LXXV.

"We may allege, thou gav'st a pledge
of thy dear Love to us,
In Wine and Bread, which figuréd
thy Grace bestowéd thus.
Of strength'ning Seals, of sweetest Meals,
have we so oft partaken;
And shall we be cast off by thee,
and utterly forsaken ?"

LXXVI.

To whom the Lord, thus in a word,
returns a short reply :
" I never knew any of you
that wrought Iniquity.

The answer.
Luke 13 : 27.
Mat. 22 : 12.

You say you've been my Presence in ;
  but then, how came you there
With Raiment vile that did defile
  and quite disgrace my Cheer ?

LXXVII.

" Durst you draw near without due fear
  Unto my holy Table ?
Durst you profane and render vain,
  so far as you were able,
Those Mysteries, which who-o prize,
  and carefully improve,
Shall savéd be undoubtedly,
  and nothing shall them move ?

LXXVIII.

" How durst you venture bold guests to enter
  in such a sordid hue,
Amongst my guests unto those Feasts
  that were not made for you ?
How durst you eat for spir'tual meat
  your bane, and drink damnation,
Whilst by your guile you render'd vile
  so rare and great Salvation ?

1 Cor. 11 : 27, 29.

LXXIX.

" Your fancies fed on heav'nly Bread,
  your hearts fed on some Lust ;
You lov'd the Creature more than th' Creator,
  your souls clove to the dust.
And think you by Hypocrisy,
  and cloakéd Wickedness,
To enter in laden with sin,
  to lasting Happiness ?

Mat. 6 : 21, 24.
Rom. 1 : 25.

LXXX.

"This your excuse shews your abuse
   of things ordain'd for good,
And doth declare you guilty are
   of my dear Flesh and Blood.
Wherefore those Seals and precious Meals
   you put so much upon
As things Divine, they Seal and Sign
   you to Perditi-on."

1 Cor. 11 : 27, 29.

LXXXI.

Then forth issue another Crew
   (those being silencéd),
Who drawing nigh to the Most High,
   adventure thus to plead :
"We sinners were," say they, "'tis clear,
   deserving condemnation ;
But did not we rely on thee,
   O Christ, for whole Salvation ?

Another sort
of Hypocrites
make their
pleas,

LXXXII.

"We did believe, and oft receive
   thy gracious Promises ;
We took great care to get a share
   in endless Happiness.
We pray'd and wept, and Fast-days kept,
   lewd ways we did eschew ;
We joyful were thy Word to hear ;
   we form'd our lives anew.

Acts 8 : 13.
Isa. 58 . 2, 3.
Heb. 6 : 4, 5.

LXXXIII.

"We thought our sin had pardon'd been,
   that our Estate was good,
Our debts all paid, our peace well made,
   our Souls wash'd with thy Blood.

2 Pet. 2 : 20.

Lord, why dost though reject us now,
    who have not thee rejected,
Nor utterly true sanctity
    and holy life neglected ?"

LXXXIV.

The Judge incens'd at their pretens'd
    self-vaunting Piety,
With such a look as trembling strook
    unto them made reply :
" O impudent, impenitent,
    and guileful generation !
Think you that I cannot descry
    your hearts' abomination ?

The Judge
urcaseth them.
John 2 : 24, 25.

LXXXV.

" You nor receiv'd, nor yet believ'd
    my Promises of Grace,
Nor were you wise enough to prize
    my reconciléd Face ;
But did presume that to assume
    which was not yours to take,
And challengéd the Children's Bread,
    yet would not sin forsake.

John 6 : 64.
Psal. 50 : 16.
Mat. 15 : 26.

LXXXVI.

" Being too bold you laid fast hold
    where int'rest you had none,
Yourselves deceiving by your believing,
    all which you might have known.
You ran away but ran astray
    with Gospel Promises,
And perishéd, being still dead
    in sins and trespasses.

Rev. 3 : 17.
Mat. 13 : 20.

LXXXVII.

"How oft did I Hypocrisy
    and Hearts' deceits unmask

Mat. 6 : 2,
4, 24.
Jer. 8 : 5, 6,
7, 8.

Before your sight, giving you light
    to know a Christian's task?
But you held fast unto the last
    your own conceits so vain,
No warning could prevail; you would
    your own Deceits retain.

LXXXVIII.

"As for your care to get a share
    in Bliss; the fear of Hell,
And of a part in endless smart,

Psal. 78 : 34,
35, 36, 37.

    did thereunto compel.
Your holiness and ways redress,
    such as it was, did spring
From no true love to things above,
    But from some other thing.

LXXXIX.

Zach. 7 : 5, 6.
Isa. 58 : 3, 4.
1 Sam. 15 :
13, 21.
Isa. 1 : 11, 15.

"You pray'd and wept, you Fast-days kept,
    but did you this to me?
No, but for sin you sought to win
    the greater liberty.
For all your vaunts, you had vile haunts,
    for which your Consciences
Did you alarm, whose voice to charm
    you us'd these practices.

XC.

"Your Penitence, your diligence

Mat. 6 : 2, 5.
John 5 : 44.

    to Read, to Pray, to Hear,
Were but to drown the clam'rous sound
    of Conscience in your Ear.

If light you lov'd, vain glory mov'd
   yourselves therewith to store,
That seeming wise men might you prize,
   and honor you the more.

XCI.

" Thus from yourselves unto yourselves,
   your duties all do tend ;   Zech. 7 : 5, 16.
And as self-love the wheels doth move,   Hos. 10 : 1.
   so in self-love they end."
Thus Christ detects their vain projects,
   and close Impiety,
And plainly shews that all their shows
   were but Hypocrisy.

XCII. ·

Then were brought nigh a Company
   of Civil honest Men,   Civil honest
That lov'd true dealing and hated stealing,   men's pleas.
   ne'er wrong'd their Brethren ;   Luke 18 : 11.
Who pleaded thus: " Thou knowest us
   that we were blameless livers ;
No Whoremongers, no Murderers,
   no quarrelers nor strivers.

XCIII.

" Idolaters, Adulterers,
   Church-robbers we were none,
Nor false dealers, nor cozeners,
   but paid each man his own.
Our way was fair, our dealing square,
   we were no wasteful spenders,
No lewd toss-pots, no drunken sots,
   no scandalous offenders.

XCIV.

"We hated vice and set great price,
    by virtuous conversation;
1 Sam. 15 : 22. And by the same we got a name
    and no small commendation.
God's Laws express that righteousness
    is that which he doth prize;
And to obey, as he doth say,
    is more than sacrifice.

XCV.

"Thus to obey hath been our way;
Eccl 7 : 20.   let our good deeds, we pray,
Find some regard and some reward
    with thee, O Lord, this day.
And whereas we transgressors be,
    of Adam's race were none,
No, not the best, but have confess'd
    themselves to have misdone."

XCVI.

Then answeréd unto their dread,
Are taken off   the Judge: "True Piety
and rendered
invalid.   God doth desire and eke require,
Deut. 10 : 12.   no less than honesty.
Tit. 2 : 12.
Jam. 2 : 10.   Justice demands at all your hands
    perfect Obedience;
If but in part you have come short,
    that is a just offense.

XCVII.

"On Earth below, where men did owe
    a thousand pounds and more,
Could twenty pence it recompense?
    Could that have clear'd the score?

Think you to buy Felicity
   with part of what's due debt?
Or for desert of one small part,
   the whole should off be set?

XCVIII.

" And yet that part whose great desert
   you think to reach so far,
For your excuse doth you accuse,
   and will your boasting mar.
However fair, however square
   your way and work hath been
Before men's eyes, yet God espies
   iniquity therein.

Luke 18: 11, 14.

XCIX.

" God looks upon th' affecti-on
   and temper of the heart;
Not only on the acti-on,
   and the external part.
Whatever end vain men pretend,
   God knows the verity,
And by the end which they intend
   their words and deeds doth try.

1 Sam. 16 : 7.
2 Chron. 25 : 2.

C.

" Without true Faith, the Scripture saith,
   God cannot take delight
In any deed that doth proceed
   from any sinful wight.
And without love all actions prove
   but barren empty things;
Dead works they be and vanity,
   the which vexation brings.

Heb. 11 : 6.
1 Cor. 13 : 1, 2, 3.

3

CI.

"Nor from true Faith, which quencheth wrath,
　　hath your obedience flown;
Nor from true Love, which wont to move
　　Believers, hath it grown.
Your argument shews your intent
　　in all that you have done;
You thought to scale Heav'n's lofty Wall
　　by Ladders of your own.

CII.

"Your blinded spirit hoping to merit
　　by your own Righteousness,
Needed no Savior but your behavior,
Rom. 10 : 3.　　and blameless carriages.
You trusted to what you could do,
　　and in no need you stood;
Your haughty pride laid me aside,
　　And trampled on my Blood.

CIII.

"All men have gone astray, and done
Rom. 9 : 30, 32.　　that which God's laws condemn;
Mat 11 : 23, 24,　But my Purchase and offer'd Grace
and 21 : 41.　　All men did not contemn.
The Ninevites and Sodomites
　　had no such sin as this;
Yet as if all your sins were small,
　　you say, 'All did amiss.'

CIV.

"Again you thought and mainly sought
　　a name with men t' acquire;
Pride bare the Bell that made you swell,
　　and your own selves admire.

Mean fruit it is, and vile, I wiss,
   that springs from such a root;
Virtue divine and genuine
   wonts not from pride to shoot.

                      Mat. 6 : 5.

CV.

" Such deeds as your are worse than poor;
   they are but sins gilt over
With silver dross, whose glist'ring gloss
   can them no longer cover.
The best of them would you condemn,
   and ruin you alone,
Although you were from faults so clear,
   that other you had none.

                      Prov. 26 : 23.
                      Mat. 23 : 27.

CVI.

" Your gold is brass, your silver dross,
   your righteousness is sin;
And think you by such honesty
   Eternal life to win ?
You much mistake, if for its sake
   you dream of acceptation;
Whereas the same deserveth shame
   and meriteth damnation."

                      Prov. 15 : 8.
                      Rom. 3 : 20.

CVII.

A wondrous crowd then 'gan aloud
   thus for themselves to say :
" We did intend, Lord, to amend,
   and to reform our way.
Our true intent was to repent
   and make our peace with thee;
But sudden death stopping our breath,
   left us no liberty.

                      Those that
                      pretend want
                      of opportunity
                      to repent.
                      Prov. 27 : 1.
                      Jam. 4 : 13.

CVIII.

"Short was our time, for in its prime
  our youthful pow'r was cropt;
We died in youth before full growth,
  so was our purpose stopt.
Let our good will to turn from ill,
  and sin to have forsaken,
Accepted be, O Lord, by thee,
  and in good part be taken."

CIX.

To whom the Judge: "Where you allege
  the shortness of the space,
That from your birth you liv'd on earth,
  to compass saving Grace,
It was Free Grace that any space
  was given you at all,
To turn from evil, defy the Devil,
  and upon God to call.

Are confuted
and convinced.
Eccl. 12 : 1.
Rev. 2 : 21.

CX.

"One day, one week wherein to seek
  God's face with all your hearts,
A favor was that far did pass
  the best of your deserts.
You had a season; what was your reason
  such precious hours to waste?
What could you find, what could you mind
  that was of greater haste?

Luke 13 : 24.
2 Cor. 6 : 2.
Heb. 3 : 7, 8, 9.

CXI.

"Could you find time for vain pastime,
  for loose, licentious mirth?
For fruitless toys and fading joys,
  that perish in the birth?

Eccl. 11 : 9
Luke 14 : 18,
19, 20.

Had you good leisure for carnal Pleasure,
in days of health and youth?
And yet no space to seek God's face,
and turn to him in truth?

CXII.

"In younger years, beyond your fears,
what if you were surprizéd?
You put away the evil day,
and of long life deviséd.
You oft were told, and might behold,
that Death no Age doth spare;
Why then did you your time foreslow,
and slight your soul's welfare?

Amos 6 : 3, 4,
5, 6.
Eph. 5 : 16.
Luke 19 : 42

CXIII.

" Had your intent been to repent,
and had you it desir'd,
There would have been endeavors seen
before your time expir'd.
God makes no treasure, nor hath he pleasure
in idle purposes;
Such fair pretenses are foul offenses,
and cloaks for wickedness."

Luke 13 : 24,
25, etc.
Phil. 2 : 12.

CXIV.

Then were brought in and charg'd with sin,
another Company,
Who by Petition obtain'd permission
to make Apology.
They arguéd, " We were misled,
as is well known to thee,
By their example that had more ample
abilities than we;

Some plead ex-
amples of their
betters.
Mat. 18 : 7.

CXV.

" Such as profess'd they did detest
    and hate each wicked way;
Whose seeming grace whilst we did trace,
    our Souls were led astray.

John 7 : 48.   When men of Parts, Learning, and Arts,
                    professing Piety,
                Did thus and thus, it seem'd to us
                    we might take liberty."

CXVI.

Who are told   The Judge replies : " I gave you eyes,
that examples
are no Rules.   And light to see your way,
Psal. 19 : 8, 11. Which had you lov'd and well improv'd,
Exod. 23 : 2.
Psal. 50 : 17,   you had not gone astray.
18.   My Word was pure, the Rule was sure ;
                        Why did you it forsake,
                Or thereon trample, and men's example
                    your Directory make ?

CXVII.

"This you well knew : that God is true,
    and that most men are liars,
2 Tim. 3 : 5.   In word professing holiness,
                    in deed thereof deniers.
                O simple fools ! that having Rules,
                    your lives to regulate,
                Would them refuse, and rather choose
                    vile men to imitate."

CXVIII.

They urge that " But, Lord," say they, " we went astray,
they were led
by godly men's   and did more wickedly,
Examples. But By means of those whom thou hast chose
all their shifts   Salvation's heirs to be."

To whom the Judge : " What you allege
    doth nothing help the case,
But makes appear how vile you were,
    and rend'reth you more base.

turn to their
greater shame.

CXIX.

" You understood that what was good,
    was to be followéd,
And that you ought that which was naught
    to have relinquishéd.
Contrariwise it was your guise
    only to imitate
Good men's defects, and their neglects
    who were regenerate.

1 Cor. 11 : 1.
Phil. 4 : 8.

CXX.

"But to express their holiness,
    or imitate their grace,
You little car'd, nor once prepar'd
    your hearts to seek my Face.
They did repent and truly rent
    their hearts for all known sin ;
You did offend, but not amend,
    to follow them therein."

Psal. 32 : 5.
2 Chron. 32 : 26.
Mat. 26 : 75.
Prov. 1 : 24, 25.

CXXI.

" We had thy Word," say some, " O Lord,
    but wiser men than we
Could never yet interpret it,
    but always disagree.
How could we fools be led by Rules
    so far beyond our ken,
Which to explain did so much pain
    and puzzle wisest men ?"

Some plead the
Scriptures'
darkness, and
difference
among Inter-
preters.
2 Pet. 3 : 16.

CXXII.

They are confuted.
Prov. 14 : 6.
Isa. 35 : 8.
Hos. 8 : 12.

" Was all my Word abstruse and hard ?"
the Judge then answered ;
" It did contain much Truth so plain
you might have run and read.
But what was hard you never car'd
to know, or studiéd ;
And things that were most plain and clear
you never practiséd.

CXXIII.

" The Mystery of Piety
Mat. 11 : 25.
Prov. 2 : 3, 4, 5.
God unto Babes reveals,
When to the Wise he it denies,
and from the world conceals.
If to fulfil God's holy Will
. had seeméd good to you,
You would have sought light as you ought,
and done the good you knew."

CXXIV.

Then came in view another crew,
and 'gan to make their pleas ;
Amongst the rest, some of the best
Others the fear
of persecution.
Acts 28 : 22.
had such poor shifts as these :
" Thou know'st right well, who all canst tell,
we liv'd amongst thy foes,
Who the Renate did sorely hate
and goodness much oppose.

CXXV.

" We holiness durst not profess,
John 12:42, 43.
fearing to be forlorn
Of all our friends, and for amends
to be the wicked's scorn.

We knew their anger would much endanger
  our lives and our estates;
Therefore, for fear, we durst appear
  no better than our mates."

CXXXVI.

To whom the Lord returns this word:
  " O wonderful deceits!
To cast off awe of God's strict law,
  and fear men's wrath and threats;
To fear hell-fire and God's fierce ire
  less than the rage of men;
As if God's wrath could do less scath
  than wrath of bretheren!

They are an-
swered.
Luke 12 : 4, 5.
Isa. 51 : 12, 13.

CXXXVII.

" To use such strife, a temp'ral life
  to rescue and secure,
And be so blind as not to mind
  that life that will endure!
This was your case, who carnal peace
  more than true joys did savor;
Who fed on dust, clave to your lust,
  and spurnéd at my favor.

CXXXVIII.

" To please your kin, men's love to win,
  to flow in worldly wealth,
To save your skin, these things have been
  more than Eternal health.
You had your choice, wherein rejoice;
  it was your porti-on,
For which you chose your souls t' expose
  unto Perditi-on.

Luke 9 : 23,
24, 25,
and 16 : 2.

3*

CXXIX.

"Who did not hate friends, life, and state,
Luke 9 : 26. with all things else for me,
Prov 8 : 36
John 3 : 19, 20. And all forsake and's Cross up-take
shall never happy be.
Well worthy they to die for aye,
who death than life had rather;
Death is their due that so value
the friendship of my Father."

CXXX.

Others plead
for pardon both
from God's
Mercy and
Justice.
Psal. 78 : 38.
2 Kin. 14 : 26. Others argue, and not a few,
"Is not God graci-ous?
His Equity and Clemency,
are they not marvellous?
Thus we believ'd; are we deceiv'd?
Cannot his Mercy great,
(As hath been told to us of old,)
assuage his anger's heat?

CXXXI.

"How can it be that God should see
his Creatures' endless pain,
Or hear their groans and rueful moans,
and still his wrath retain?
Can it agree with Equity,
can Mercy have the heart,
To recompense few years' offense
with everlasting smart?

CXXXII.

"Can God delight in such a sight
as sinners' misery?
Psal. 30 : 9.
Mic. 7 : 18. Or what great good can this our blood
bring unto the most High?

O thou that dost thy Glory most
   in pard'ning sin display,
Lord, might it please thee to release
   and pardon us this day!

CXXXIII.

" Unto thy name more glorious fame
   would not such Mercy bring?
Would not it raise thine endless praise,
   more than our suffering?"
With that they cease, holding their peace,
   but cease not still to weep;
Grief ministers a flood of tears,
   in which their words do steep.

CXXXIV.

But all too late; grief's out of date,
   when Life is at an end.   ~   They are
                                      answered.
The glorious King thus answering,
   all to his voice attend:
" God gracious is," quoth he; " like his,
   no mercy can be found:
His Equity and Clemency
   to sinners do abound,

CXXXV.

" As may appear by those that here   Mercy now
   are plac'd at my right hand,   shines forth in
                                      the vessels of
Whose stripes I bore, and clear'd the score,   Mercy.
   that they might quitted stand.   Mic. 7 : 18
                                      Rom. 9 : 23.
For surely none but God alone,
   whose Grace transcends men's thought,
For such as those that were his foes
   like wonders would have wrought.

CXXXVI.

Did also wait
upon such as
abused it.
Rom. 2 : 4.
Hos. 11 : 4.

" And none but he such lenity
    and patience would have shown
To you so long, who did him wrong,
    and pull'd his Judgment down.
How long a space, O stiff-neck'd race,
    did patience you afford ?
How oft did love you gently move,
    to turn unto the Lord ?

CXXXVII.

" With chords of love God often strove
Luke 13 : 34.
The day of
Grace now past   your stubborn hearts to tame ;
Nevertheless your wickedness
    did still resist the same.
If now at last Mercy be past
    from you for evermore,
And Justice come in Mercy's room,
    yet grudge you not therefore.

CXXXVIII.

"If into wrath God turnéd hath
    his long, long-suffering,
Luke 19 : 42,
43.
Jude 4. And now for love you vengeance prove,
    it is an equal thing.
Your waxing worse hath stopt the course
    of wonted Clemency,
Mercy refus'd and Grace misus'd
    call for severity.

CXXXIX.

" It's now high time that ev'ry Crime
Rom. 2 : 5, 6.
Isa. 1 : 24.
Amos 2 : 13,
Gen. 18 : 25.   be brought to punishment ;
Wrath long contain'd and oft restrain'd,
    at last must have a vent.

Justice severe cannot forbear
　　to plague sin any longer,
But must inflict with hand most strict
　　mischief upon the wronger.

CXL.

" In vain do they for Mercy pray,
　　the season being past,
Who had no care to get a share
　　therein, while time did last.
The man whose ear refus'd to hear
　　the voice of Wisdom's cry,
Earn'd this reward, that none regard
　　him in his misery.

Mat. 25 : 3, 1, 2.
Prov. 12 : 8, 29, 30.

CXLI.

" It doth agree with Equity
　　and with God's holy Law,
That those should die eternally
　　that Death upon them draw.
The soul that sins Damnation wins,
　　for so the Law ordains ;
Which Law is just ; and therefore must
　　such suffer endless pains.

Isa. 5 : 18, 19.
Gen. 2 : 17.
Rom. 2 : 8, 9.

CXLII.

" Eternal smart is the desert
　　ev'n of the least offense ;
Then wonder not if I allot
　　to you this Recompense ;
But wonder more that since so sore
　　and lasting plagues are due
To every sin, you liv'd therein,
　　who well the danger knew.

Rom. 6 : 23.
2 Thes. 1 : 8, 9.

CXLIII.

Ezek. 33 : 11.
Exod. 34 : 7,
and 11 : 17.

" God hath no joy to crush or 'stroy,
   and ruin wretched wights;
But to display the glorious Ray
   of Justice he delights.
To manifest he doth detest,
   and throughly hate all sin,

Rom. 9 : 22.

By plaguing it as is most fit—
   this shall him Glory win."

CXLIV.

Some pretend
they were shut
out of Heaven
by God's
Decree.
Rom. 9 : 18, 19.

Then at the Bar arraignéd are
   an impudenter sort,
Who to evade the guilt that's laid
   Upon them, thus retort :
" How could we cease thus to transgress ?
   How could we Hell avoid,
Whom God's Decree shut out from thee,
   and sign'd to be destroy'd ?

CXLV.

" Whom God ordains to endless pains
   by Law unalterable,

Heb. 22 : 17.
Rom. 11 : 7, 8.

Repentance true, Obedience new,
   to save such are unable.
Sorrow for sin no good can win,
   to such as are rejected ;
Nor can they grieve nor yet believe,
   that never were elected.

CXLVI.

" Of Man's fall'n race, who can true Grace
   or Holiness obtain ?
Who can convert or change his heart,
   if God withhold the same ?

Had we applied ourselves and tried
  as much as who did most,
God's love to gain, our busy pain
  and labor had been lost."

CXLVII.

Christ readily makes this Reply:
  "I damn you not because
You are rejected, nor yet elected;
  but you have broke my Laws.
It is in vain your wits to strain
  the end and means to sever;
Men fondly seek to part or break
  what God hath link'd together.

Their pleas taken off.
Luke 13 : 27.
2 Pet. 1 : 9, 10,
compared with
Mat. 19 : 16.

CXLVIII.

"Whom God will save, such he will have
  the means of life to use;
Whom he'll pass by shall choose to die,
  and ways of life refuse.
He that fore-sees and fore-decrees,
  in wisdom order'd has,
That man's free-will, electing ill,
  shall bring his Will to pass.

Acts 3 : 19,
and 16 : 31.
1 Sam. 2 : 15.
John 3 : 19.
Job 5 : 40.
2 Thes. 2 : 11,
12.

CXLIX.

"High God's Decree, as it is free,
  so doth it none compel
Against their will to good or ill;
  it forceth none to Hell.
They have their wish whose Souls perish
  with Torments in Hell-fire,
Who rather choose their souls to lose,
  than leave a loose desire.

Ezek. 33 : 11,
12.
Luke 13 : 34.
Prov. 8 : 33,
36.

CL.

Gen. 2 : 17.
Mat. 25 : 41,
42.
Ezek. 18 : 20.

" God did ordain sinners to pain,
    yet he to Hell sends none
But such as swerv'd and have deserv'd
    destruction as their own.
His pleasure is, that none from Bliss
    and endless happiness
Be barr'd, but such as wrong'd him much,
    by willful wickedness.

CLI.

2 Pet. 1 : 10.
Acts 13 : 46.
Luke 13 : 24.

" You, sinful Crew! no other knew
    but you might be elect;
Why did you then yourselves condemn?
    Why did you me reject?
Where was your strife to gain that life
    which lasteth evermore?
You never knock'd, yet say God lock'd
    against you Heaven's door.

CLII.

Mat. 7 : 7, 8

" 'Twas no vain task to knock and ask,
    whilst life continuéd.
Who ever sought Heav'n as he ought,
    and seeking perishéd?
The lowly, meek, who truly seek
    for Christ and for Salvation,
There's no decree whereby such be
    ordain'd to condemnation.

Gal. 5 : 22, 23.

CLIII.

" You argue then: ' But abject men,
    whom God resolves to spill,
Cannot repent, nor their hearts rent;
    nor can they change their will.'

Not for his *Can* is any man
   adjudgéd unto Hell,
But for his *Will* to do what's ill,   John 3 : 19.
   and nilling to do well.

CLIV.

"I often stood tend'ring my Blood
   to wash away your guilt,
And eke my Sprite to frame you right,
   lest your Souls should be spilt.
But you, vile Race, rejected Grace,   John 5 : 40.
   when Grace was freely proffer'd,
No changéd heart, no heav'nly part
   would you, when it was offer'd.

CLV.

"Who willfully the remedy,
   and means of life contemnéd,
Cause have the same themselves to blame,   John 15 : 22,
   if now they be condemnéd.   24.
                                 Heb. 2 : 3.
You have yourselves, you and none else,   Isa. 66 : 34.
   to blame that you must die ;
You chose the way to your decay,
   and perish'd willfully."

CLVI.

These words appall and daunt them all,
   dismay'd and all amort,
Like stocks that stand at Christ's left hand
   and dare no more retort.
Then were brought near with trembling fear,
   a number numberless,
Of Blind Heathen and brutish men,
   that did God's Law transgress ;

CLVII.

Whose wicked ways Christ open lays,
   and makes their sins appear,
They making pleas their case to ease,
   if not themselves to clear.

Heathen men plead want of the Written Word.

"Thy Written Word," say they, "good Lord,
   we never did enjoy;
We ne'er refus'd, nor it abus'd;
   Oh, do not us destroy!"

CLVIII.

"You ne'er abus'd, nor yet refus'd
   my Written Word, you plead;
That's true," quoth he, "therefore shall ye
   the less be punishéd.

Mat. 11 : 22.
Luke 12 : 48.

You shall not smart for any part
   of other men's offense,
But for your own transgressi-on
   receive due recompense."

CLIX.

"But we were blind," say they, "in mind;
   too dim was Nature's Light,
Our only guide, as hath been tried,
   to bring us to the sight

1 Cor. 1 : 21,
Insufficiency of the light of Nature.

Of our estate degenerate,
   and curs'd by Adam's Fall;
How we were born and lay forlorn
   in bondage and in thrall.

CLX.

"We did not know a Christ till now,
   nor how fall'n men be savéd,
Else would we not, right well we wot,
   have so ourselves behavéd.

We should have mourn'd, we should have turn'd
    from sin at thy Reproof,
And been more wise through thy advice,
    for our own soul's behoof.   Mat. 11 : 22.

CLXI.

" But Nature's light shin'd not so bright,
    to teach us the right way :
We might have lov'd it and well improv'd it,
    and yet have gone astray."
The Judge most High makes this Reply :   They are
    " You ignorance pretend,   answered.
Dimness of sight, and want of light,
    your course Heav'nward to bend.

CLXII.

" How came your mind to be so blind ?
    I once you knowledge gave,
Clearness of sight and judgment right :   Gen. 1 : 27.
    who did the same deprave ?   Eccl. 7 : 29.
                                 Hos. 13 : 9.
If to your cost you have it lost,
    and quite defac'd the same,
Your own desert hath caus'd the smart ;
    you ought not me to blame.

CLXIII.

" Yourselves into a pit of woe,
    your own transgression led ;   Mat. 11 : 25,
If I to none my Grace had shown,   compared with
    who had been injuréd ?   20 : 15.
If to a few, and not to you,
    I shew'd a way of life,
My Grace so free, you clearly see,
    gives you no ground of strife.

CLXIV.

"'Tis vain to tell, you wot full well,
  if you in time had known
Your misery and remedy,
  your actions had it shown :
Rom. 1 : 20, You, sinful Crew, have not been true
21, 22.   unto the Light of Nature,
Nor done the good you understood,
  nor ownéd your Creator.

CLXV.

"He that the Light, because 'tis slight,
  hath uséd to despise,
Rom. 2 : 12, 15, Would not the Light shining more bright,
and 1 : 32.   be likely for to prize.
Mat. 12 : 41.
If you had lov'd, and well improv'd
  your knowledge and dim sight,
Herein your pain 'had not been vain,
  your plagues had been more light."

CLXVI.

Reprobate In- Then to the Bar all they drew near
fants plead for   Who died in infancy,
themselves.
Rev. 20 : 12, And never had or good or bad
15,   effected pers'nally ;
compared with
Rom. 5 : 12, 14, But from the womb unto the tomb
and 9 : 11, 13.   were straightway carriéd,
Ezek. 18 : 2.
(Or at the least ere they transgress'd)
  who thus began to plead :

CLXVII.

"If for our own transgressi-on,
  or disobedience,
We here did stand at thy left hand,
  just were the Recompense ;

But Adam's guilt our souls hath spilt,
  his fault is charg'd upon us;
And that alone hath overthrown
  and utterly undone us.

CLXVIII.

" Not we, but he ate of the Tree,
  whose fruit was interdicted;
Yet on us all of his sad Fall
  the punishment's inflicted.
How could we sin that had not been,
  or how is his sin our,
Without consent, which to prevent
  we never had the pow'r ?

CLXIX.

" O great Creator why was our Nature
  depravéd and forlorn ?
Why so defil'd, and made so vil'd,
  whilst we were yet unborn ?
If it be just, and needs we must
  transgressors reckon'd be,
Thy Mercy, Lord, to us afford,   Psal. 51 : 5.
  which sinners hath set free.

CLXX.

" Behold we see Adam set free,
  and sav'd from his trespass;
Whose sinful Fall hath split us all,
  and brought us to this pass.
Canst thou deny us once to try,
  or Grace to us to tender,
When he finds grace before thy face,
  who was the chief offender ?"

CLXXI.

Then answeréd the Judge most dread :
Their argu-
ments taken off.
Ezek. 18 : 20.
Rom. 5 : 12, 19. "God doth such doom forbid,
That men should die eternally
  for what they never did.
But what you call old Adam's Fall,
  and only his Trespass,
You call amiss to call it his,
  both his and yours it was.

CLXXII.

"He was design'd of all Mankind
  to be a public Head ;
1 Cor. 15
48, 49. A common Root, whence all should shoot,
  and stood in all their stead.
He stood and fell, did ill or well,
  not for himself alone,
But for you all, who now his Fall
  and trespass would disown.

CLXXIII.

"If he had stood, then all his brood
  had been establishéd
In God's true love never to move,
  nor once awry to tread ;
Then all his Race my Father's Grace
  should have enjoy'd for ever,
And wicked Sprites by subtile sleights
  could them have harméd never.

CLXXIV.

Would you have griev'd to have receiv'd
  through Adam so much good,
As had been your for evermore,
  if he at first had stood ?

Would you have said, 'We ne'er obey'd
   nor did thy laws regard ;
It ill befits with benefits,
   us, Lord, to so reward ?'

CLXXV.

" Since then to share in his welfare,
   you could have been content,
You may with reason share in his treason,
   and in the punishment.
Hence you were born in state forlorn,
   with Natures so depravéd ;
Death was your due because that you
   had thus yourselves behavéd.

Rom. 5 : 12.
Psal. 51 : 5.
Gen. 5 : 3.

CLXXVI.

" You think ' If we had been as he,
   whom God did so betrust,
We to our cost would ne'er have lost
   all for a paltry lust.'
Had you been made in Adam's stead,
   you would like things have wrought,
And so into the self-same woe,
   yourselves and yours have brought.

Mat. 23: 30, 31.

CLXXVII.

" I may deny you once to try,
   or Grace to you to tender,
Though he finds Grace before my face
   who was the chief offender ;
Else should my Grace cease to be Grace,
   for it would not be free,
If to release whom I should please
   I have no liberty.

Rom. 9 : 15, 18.
The free gift.
Rom. 5 : 15.

CLXXVIII.

" If upon one what's due to none
I frankly shall bestow,
And on the rest shall not think best
compassion's skirt to throw,
Whom injure I? will you envy
and grudge at others' weal?
Or me accuse, who do refuse
yourselves to help and heal?

CLXXIX.

" Am I alone of what's my own,
no Master or no Lord?
Mat. 20 : 15. And if I am, how can you claim
what I to some afford?
Will you demand Grace at my hand,
and challenge what is mine?
Will you teach me whom to set free,
and thus my Grace confine?

CLXXX.

Psal. 58 : 8. " You sinners are, and such a share
Rom. 6 : 23.
Gal. 3 : 10.   as sinners, may expect;
Rom. 8 : 29, Such you shall have, for I do save
30, and 11 : 7.
Rev. 21 : 27.   none but mine own Elect.
Luke 12 : 14, 8. Yet to compare your sin with their
Mat. 11 : 22.   who liv'd a longer time,
I do confess yours is much less,
though every sin's a crime.

CLXXXI.

The wicked all " A crime it is, therefore in bliss
convinced and
put to silence.   you may not hope to dwell;
Rom. 3 : 19. But unto you I shall allow
Mat. 22 : 12.   the easiest room in Hell."

The glorious King thus answering,
  they cease, and plead no longer ;
Their Consciences must needs confess
  his Reasons are the stronger.

CLXXXII.

Thus all men's pleas the Judge with ease
  doth answer and confute,
Until that all, both great and small,
  are silencéd and mute.
Vain hopes are cropt, all mouths are stopt,
  sinners have naught to say,
But that 'tis just and equal most
  they should be damn'd for aye.

Behold the formidable estate of all the ungodly as they stand hopeless and helpless before an impartial Judge, expecting their final Sentence. Rev. 6 : 16, 17.

CLXXXIII.

Now what remains, but that to pains
  and everlasting smart,
Christ should condemn the sons of men,
  which is their just desert ?
Oh rueful plights of sinful wights !
  Oh wretches all forlorn !
'T had happy been they ne'er had seen
  the sun, or not been born.

CLXXXIV.

Yea now it would be good they could
  themselves annihilate,
And cease to be, themselves to free
  from such a fearful state.
O happy Dogs, and Swine, and Frogs,
  yea, Serpent's generation !
Who do not fear this doom to hear,
  and sentence of Damnation !

CLXXXV.

This is their state so desperate;
   their sins are fully known;
Their vanities and villanies

Psal. 139 : 2, 3,   before the world are shown.
4.
Eccl. 12 : 14.   As they are gross and impious,
   so are their numbers more
Than motes in th' Air, or than their hair,
   or sands upon the shore.

CLXXXVI.

Divine Justice offended is,
   and satisfaction claimeth;
God's wrathful ire, kindled like fire,

Mat. 25 : 45.   against them fiercely flameth.
Their Judge severe doth quite cashier,
   and all their pleas off take,
That ne'er a man, or dare, or can
   a further answer make.

CLXXXVII.

Their mouths are shut, each man is put

Mat. 22 : 12.   to silence and to shame,
Rom.2 : 5, 6.
Luke 19 : 42.   Nor have they aught within their thought,
   Christ's Justice for to blame.
The Judge is just, and plague them must,
   nor will he Mercy shew,
For Mercy's day is past away
   to any of this Crew.

CLXXXVIII.

The Judge is strong, doers of wrong

Mat. 28 : 18.   cannot his pow'r withstand;
None can by flight run out of sight,
   nor 'scape out of his hand.

Sad is their state; for Advocate,
  to plead their cause, there's none; Psal. 137 : 7·
None to prevent their punishment,
  or mis'ry to bemoan.

CLXXXIX.

O dismal day! whither shall they
  for help and succor flee?
To God above with hopes to move
  their greatest Enemy? Isa. 33 : 14.
His wrath is great, whose burning heat Psal. 11 : 6.
  no floods of tears can slake; Num. 25 : 19.
His Word stands fast that they be cast
  into the burning Lake.

CXC

To Christ their Judge? He doth adjudge Mat. 25 : 41,
  them to the Pit of Sorrow; and 25 : 10, 11,
Nor will he hear, or cry or tear, 12.
  nor respite them one morrow.
To Heav'n, alas! they cannot pass,
  it is against them shut;
To enter there (O heavy cheer)
  they out of hopes are put.

CXCI.

Unto their Treasures, or to their Pleasures? Luke 12 : 20.
  All these have them forsaken; Psal. 49 : 7, 17.
Had they full coffers to make large offers, Deut. 32 : 2.
  their gold would not be taken.
Unto the place where whilom was
  their birth and Education?
Lo! Christ begins for their great sins,
  to fire the Earth's Foundation;

CXCII.

And by and by the flaming Sky
   shall drop like molten Lead
About their ears, t' increase their fears,
2 Pet. 3 : 10.   and aggravate their dread.
To Angel's good that ever stood
   in their integrity,
Should they betake themselves, and make
   their suit incessantly ?

CXCIII.

They've neither skill, nor do they will
   to work them any ease ;
They will not mourn to see them burn,
Mat. 13 : 41, 42.   nor beg for their release.
Rev. 20 : 13, 15. To wicked men, their brethren
   in sin and wickedness,
Should they make moan ?   Their case is one ;
   they're in the same distress.

CXCIV.

Ah ! cold comfort and mean support,
   from such like Comforters !
Ah ! little joy of Company,
Luke 16 : 28.   and fellow-sufferers !
Such shall increase their heart's disease,
   and add unto their woe,
Because that they brought to decay
   themselves and many moe.

CXCV.

Unto the Saints with sad complaints
   should they themselves apply ?
Rev. 21 : 4. They're not dejected nor aught affected
Psal. 58 : 10.   with all their misery.

Friends stand aloof and make no proof
  what Prayers or Tears can do ;
Your Godly friends are now more friends
  to Christ than unto you.

CXCVI.

Where tender love men's hearts did move
  unto a sympathy,
And bearing part of others' smart
  in their anxiety,   1 Cor. 6 : 2.
Now such compassion is out of fashion,
  and wholly laid aside ;
No friends so near, but Saints to hear
  their Sentence can abide.

CXCVII.

One natural Brother beholds another
  in his astonied fit,
Yet sorrows not thereat a jot,   Compare
  nor pities him a whit.   Prov. 1 : 26.
                                   with 1 John 3 :
The godly Wife conceives no grief,   2, and 2 Cor.
  nor can she shed a tear   5 : 16.
For the sad state of her dear Mate,
  when she his doom doth hear.

CXCVIII.

He that was erst a Husband pierc'd
  with sense of Wife's distress,
Whose tender heart did bear a part
  of all her grievances,
Shall mourn no more as heretofore,
  because of her ill plight,
Although he see her now to be
  a damn'd forsaken wight.

CXCIX.

The tender Mother will own no other
of all her num'rous brood,
But such as stand at Christ's right hand,
Luke 16 : 25.   acquitted through his Blood.
The pious Father had now much rather
his graceless Son should lie
In Hell with Devils, for all his evils,
burning eternally,

CC.

Than God most High should injury
by sparing him sustain ;
Psal. 58 : 10.   And doth rejoice to hear Christ's voice,
adjudging him to pain.
Thus having all, both great and small,
convinc'd and silencéd,
Christ did proceed their Doom to read,
and thus it utteréd :

CCI.

The Judge pronounceth the sentence of condemnation. Mat. 25 : 41.

"Ye sinful wights and curséd sprights,
that work iniquity,
Depart together from me for ever
to endless Misery ;
Your portion take in yonder Lake,
where Fire and Brimstone flameth ;
Suffer the smart which your desert,
as its due wages claimeth."

CCII.

The terror of it.

Oh piercing words, more sharp than swords !
What ! to depart from Thee,
Whose face before for evermore
the best of Pleasures be !

What ! to depart (unto our smart),
   from thee *Eternally !*
To be for aye banish'd away
   with Devils' company !

CCIII.

What ! to be sent to Punishment,
   and flames of burning Fire !
To be surrounded, and eke confounded
   with God's revengeful Ire !
What ! to abide, not for a tide,
   these Torments, but for Ever !
To be releas'd, or to be eas'd,
   not after years, but Never !

CCIV.

Oh fearful Doom ! now there's no room
   for hope or help at all ;
Sentence is past which aye shall last ;
   Christ will not it recall.
Then might you hear them rend and tear
   the Air with their out-cries ;
The hideous noise of their sad voice
   ascendeth to the Skies.

CCV.

They wring their hands, their caitiff-hands,
   and gnash their teeth for terror ;   Luke 13 : 38.
They cry, they roar for anguish sore,   Prov. 1 : 26.
   and gnaw their tongues for horror.
But get away without delay,
   Christ pities not your cry ;
Depart to Hell, there may you yell,
   and roar Eternally.

CCVI.

That word *"Depart,"* maugre their heart,
 drives every wicked one,
With mighty pow'r, the self-same hour,
 far from the Judge's Throne.
Away they're chas'd by the strong blast
 of his Death-threat'ning mouth;
They flee full fast, as if in haste,
 although they be full loath.

It is put in
Execution.
Mat. 25 : 46.

CCVII.

As chaff that's dry, as dust doth fly
 before the Northern wind,
Right so are they chaséd away,
 and can no Refuge find.
They hasten to the Pit of Woe,
 guarded by Angels stout,
Who to fulfil Christ's holy Will,
 attend this wickéd Rout;

Mat. 13 : 41, 42.

CCVIII.

Whom having brought as they are taught,
 unto the brink of Hell,
(That dismal place, far from Christ s face,
 where Death and Darkness dwell,
Where God's fierce Ire kindleth the fire,
 and vengeance feeds the flame,
With piles of Wood and Brimstone Flood,
 so none can quench the same,)

Hell.
Mat. 25 : 30,
Mark 9 : 42.
Isa. 30 : 33.
Rev. 21 : 8.

CCIX.

With Iron bands they bind their hands
 and curséd feet together,
And cast them all, both great and small,
 into that Lake forever,

Wicked men
and Devils cast
into it forever.
Mat. 22 : 13,
and 25 : 46.

Where day and night, without respite,
   they wail, and cry and howl,
For tort'ring pain which they sustain,
   in Body and in Soul.

CCX.

For day and night, in their despite,   Rev. 14 : 10, 11.
   their torment's smoke ascendeth,
Their pain and grief have no relief,
   their anguish never endeth.
There must they lie and never die,
   though dying every day ;
There must they dying ever lie,
   and not consume away.

CCXI.

Die fain they would if die they could,
   but Death will not be had ;
God's direful wrath their bodies hath
   forev'r immortal made.
They live to lie in misery,
   and bear eternal woe ;
And live they must whilst God is just,
   that he may plague them so.

CCXII.

But who can tell the plagues of Hell,   The unsuffera-
   and torments exquisite ?   ble torments of
Who can relate their dismal state,   the Damned.
   and terrors infinite ?   Luke 16 24.
Who fare the best and feel the least,   Jude 7.
   yet feel that punishment
Whereby to nought they would be brought
   if God did not prevent.

CCXIII.

The least degree of misery
   there felt is incomparable;

Isa. 33 : 14.
Mark 9 : 43, 44.
The lightest pain they there sustain
   is more than intolerable.
But God's great pow'r from hour to hour
   upholds them in the fire,
That they shall not consume a jot
   nor by its force expire.

CCXIV.

But, ah, the woe they undergo
   (*they* more than all beside)
Who had the light, and knew the right,
Luke 12 : 47.
   yet would not it abide !
The sev'n fold smart which to their part
   and porti-on doth fall,
Who Christ's free Grace would not embrace,
   nor hearken to his call.

CCXV.

The Amorites and Sodomites,
Mat. 11 : 24.
   although their plagues be sore,
Yet find some ease compar'd to these,
   who feel a great deal more.
Almighty God, whose Iron Rod,
   to smite them never lins,
Doth most declare his Justice rare
   in plaguing these men's sins.

CCXVI.

The pain of loss their souls doth toss,
Luke 16 : 23,
25, and 13 : 28.
   and wond'rously distress,
To think what they have cast away
   by willful wickedness.

" We might have been redeem'd from sin,"
   think they, "and liv'd above,
Being possesst of Heav'nly rest,
   and joying in God's love.

CCXVII.

" But woe, woe, woe, our Souls unto!
   we would not happy be ;
And therefore bear God's vengeance here   Luke 13 : 24.
   to all Eternity.
Experience and woful sense
   must be our painful teachers,
Who'd not believe, nor credit give
   unto our faithful Preachers."

CCXVIII.

Thus shall they lie and wail and cry,
   tormented and tormenting ;
Their galléd hearts with poison'd darts,   Mat. 9 : 44.
   but now too late repenting.   Rom. 2 : 15.
There let them dwell in th' Flames of Hell :
   there leave we them to burn,
And back again unto the men
   whom Christ acquits, return.

CCXIX.

The Saints behold with courage bold   The Saints
   and thankful wonderment,   rejoice to see
To see all those that were their foes   Judgment exe-
   thus sent to punishment.   cuted upon the
Then do they sing unto their King   Wicked World.
   a Song of endless Praise ;   Psal. 58 : 10.
They praise his Name and do proclaim   Rev. 10 : 1,
   that just are all his ways.   2, 3.

CCXX.

They ascend
with Christ in-
to Heaven tri-
umphing.
Mat. 25 : 46.

Thus with great joy and melody
  to Heav'n they all ascend,
Him there to praise with sweetest lays,
  and Hymns that never end;
Where with long rest they shall be blest,
  and naught shall them annoy,
Where they shall see as seen they be,
  and whom they love enjoy.

CCXXI.

1 John 3 : 2.
1 Cor. 13 12.
Their eternal
happiness and
incomparable
glory there.

Oh glorious Place ! where face to face ⬤
  Jehovah may be seen,
By such as were sinners while here,
  and no dark veil between !
Where the Sunshine and light Divine
  of God's bright countenance,
Doth rest upon them every one,
  with sweetest influence !

CCXXII.

Oh blessed state of the Renate !
  Oh wond'rous happiness,
To which they're brought beyond what thought
Rev. 21 : 4.   can reach or words express !
Grief's watercourse and sorrow's source
  are turn'd to joyful streams;
Their old distress and heaviness
  are vanishéd like dreams.

CCXXIII.

For God above in arms of love
  doth dearly them embrace,
Psal. 16 : 11.   And fills their sprights with such delights,
  and pleasures in his Grace,

As shall not fail, nor yet grow stale,
   through frequency of use ;
Nor do they fear God's favor there
   to forfeit by abuse.

CCXXIV.

For there the Saints are perfect Saints,
   and holy ones indeed ;
From all the sin that dwelt within   Heb. 12 : 23.
   their mortal bodies freed ;
Made Kings and Priests to God through Christ's
   dear Love's transcendency,
There to remain and there to reign   Rev. 1 : 6,
   with him Eternally.   and 22 : 5.

A SHORT DISCOURSE ON ETERNITY.

WHAT mortal man can with a Span
  mete out Eternity?
Or fathom it by depth of Wit,
  or strength of Memory?
The lofty Sky is not so high,
  Hell's depth to this is small;
The World so wide is but a stride,
  comparéd therewithal.

It is a main great Oce-an
  withouten bank or bound,
A deep Abyss, wherein there is
  no bottom to be found.
This World hath stood now since the Flood,
  four thousand years well near,
And had before enduréd more
  than sixteen hundred year.

But what's the time from the World's prime,
  unto this present day,
If we thereby Eternity
  to measure should essay?
The whole duration since the Creation,
  though long, yet is more little,
If placed by Eternity,
  than is the smallest tittle.

Tell every Star both near and far,
   in Heav'n's bright Canopy
That doth appear throughout the year
   of high or low degree:
Tell every Tree that thou canst see
   in this vast Wilderness,
Up in the Woods, down by the Floods,
   in thousand miles Progress :

The sum is vast, yet not so vast
   but that thou may'st go on
To multiply the leaves thereby,
   that hang those Trees upon :
Add thereunto the Drops that thou
   imaginest to be
In April Show'rs, that bring forth Flow'rs
   and blossoms plenteously :

Number the Fowls and living Souls
   that through the Air do fly,
The wingéd Hosts in all their Coasts
   beneath the starry Sky :
Count all the Grass as thou dost pass
   through many a pasture-land,
And dewy Drops that on the tops
   of Herbs and Plants do stand :

Number the Sand upon the Strand,
   and atoms of the Air;
And do thy best on Man and Beast,
   to reckon every Hair :
Take all the Dust, if so thou lust,
   and add to thine Account :
Yet shall the Years of Sinners' tears,
   the Number far surmount.

Naught join'd to naught can ne'er make aught,
   nor Cyphers make a Sum;
Nor things finite, to infinite
   by multiplying come:
A Cockle-shell may serve as well
   to lade the Ocean dry
As finite things and reckonings
   to bound Eternity.

Oh happy they that live for aye,
   with Christ in Heav'n above!
Who know withal that nothing shall
   deprive them of his love.
Eternity, Eternity!
   Oh! were it not for thee,
The Saints in bliss and happiness
   could never happy be.

For if they were in any fear
   that this their joy might cease,
It would annoy (if not destroy)
   and interrupt their peace.
But being sure it shall endure
   so long as God shall live;
The thoughts of this, unto their bliss,
   do full perfection give.

Cheer up ye Saints amidst your wants
   and sorrows many a one;
Lift up the head, shake off all dread,
   and moderate your moan.
Your sufferings and evil things
   will suddenly be past;
Your sweet Fruitions and blessed Visions,
   for evermore shall last.

Lament and mourn you that must burn
　　amidst those flaming Seas :
If once you come to such a doom,
　　for ever farewell ease.
O sad estate and desperate,
　　that never can be mended,
Until God's Will shall change, or till
　　Eternity be ended !

If any one this Questi-on
　　shall unto me propound :
What ! have the years of Sinners' tears
　　no limits or no bound ?
It kills our heart to think of smart,
　　and pains that last for ever ;
And hear of fire that shall expire,
　　or be extinguish'd never,

I'll answer make (and let them take
　　my words as I intend them ;
For this is all the Cordi-al
　　that here I have to lend them :)
When Heav'n shall cease to flow with peace
　　and all felicity,
Then Hell may cease to be the place
　　of Woe and Misery.

When Heav'n is Hell, when Ill is Well,
　　when Virtue turns to Vice ;
When Wrong is Right, when Dark is Light,
　　when Naught is of great price ;
Then may the years of Sinners' tears
　　and sufferings expire,
And all the Hosts of damnéd Ghosts
　　escape out of Hell-fire.

When Christ above shall cease to love,
　　when God shall cease to reign
And be no more as heretofore
　　the World's great Sovéreign;
Or not be just, or favor lust,
　　or in Men's sins delight;
Then wicked men (and not till then)
　　to Heav'n may take their flight.

When God's great Power shall be brought lower,
　　by foreign Puissance,
Or be decay'd and weaker made
　　through Time's continuance;
When drowsiness shall him oppress,
　　and lay him fast asleep,
Then sinful men may break their pen,
　　and out of Prison creep.

When those in Glory shall be right sorry
　　they may not change their place,
And wish to dwell with those in Hell,
　　never to see Christ's face;
Then those in pain may freedom gain
　　and be with Glory dight:
Then Hellish fiends may be Christ's Friends,
　　and Heirs of Heavén hight.

Then, ah! poor men! What! not till then?
　　No, not an hour before;
For God is just, and therefore must
　　torment them evermore.
ETERNITY! ETERNITY!
　　thou mak'st hard hearts to bleed:
The thoughts of thee in misery,
　　do make men wail indeed.

When they remind what's still behind
  and ponder this word NEVER,
That they must there be made to bear
  God's Vengéance for EVER :
The thought of this more bitter is
  than all they feel beside ;
Yet what they feel, nor heart of steel,
  nor flesh of brass can bide.

To lie in woe and undergo
  the direful pains of Hell,
And know withal, that there they shall
  for aye and ever dwell ;   .
And that they are from rest as far
  · when fifty thousand year,
· Twice told, are spent in punishment,
  as when they first came there ;

This, oh ! this makes Hell's fiery flakes
  much more intolerable ;
This makes frail wights and damnéd sprites
  to bear their plagues unable.
This makes men bite, for fell despite,
  their very tongues in twain ;
This makes them roar for great horror,
  and trebleth all their pain.

A POSTSCRIPT UNTO THE READER.

AND now, good Reader, I return again
To talk with thee who hast been at the pain
To read throughout and heed what went before;
And unto thee I'll speak a little more.
Give ear I pray thee unto what I say,
That God may hear thy voice another day.
Thou hast a Soul, my Friend, and so have I,
To save or lose; a Soul that cannot die;
A Soul of greater price than Gold or Gems;
A Soul more worth than Crowns and Diadems;
A Soul at first created like its Maker,
And of God's Image made to be partaker:
Upon the wings of noblest Faculties,
Taught for to soar above the Starry Skies,
And not to rest, until it understood
Itself possesséd of the chiefest Good.
And since the Fall thy Soul retaineth still
Those faculties of Reason and of Will,
But oh! how much deprav'd and out of frame,
As if they were some other's, not the same!
Thine Understanding dismally benighted,
And Reason's eye in Spir'tual things dim-sighted,
Or else stark blind; thy Will inclin'd to evil,
And nothing else; a slave unto the Devil;
That loves to live, and liveth to transgress,
But shuns the way of God and Holiness.

All thine Affections are disordered,
And thus by headstrong Passions are misled.
What need I tell thee of thy crooked way,
And many wicked wand'rings every day?
Or that thine own transgressi-ons are more
In number than the sands upon the Shore?
Thou art a lump of wickedness become,
And may'st with horror think upon thy Doom,
Until thy Soul be washéd in the flood
Of Christ's most dear, soul-cleansing, precious Blood.
That, that alone can do away thy sin,
Which thou wert born and hast long livéd in;
That, only that can pacify God's wrath,
If apprehended by a lively Faith,
Now whilst the day and means of Grace do last,
Before the opportunity be past.

But if, O man, thou liv'st a Christless creature,
And Death surprise thee in a state of nature,
(As who can tell but that may be thy case?)
How wilt thou stand before the Judge's face,
When he shall be reveal'd in flaming fire,
And come to pay ungodly men their hire,
To execute due vengeance upon those
That knew him not, or that had been his foes?
What wilt thou answer unto his demands,
When he requires a reason at thy hands,
Of all the things that thou hast said or done,
Or left undone, or set thine heart upon?
When he shall thus with thee expostulate:
" What cause hadst thou thy Maker for to hate,
To take up arms against thy Sovéreign,
And enmity against him to maintain?
What injury hath God Almighty done thee?

What good hath he withheld that might have won thee?
What evil, or injustice hast thou found
In him that might unto thine hurt redound?
If neither felt nor feared injury
Hath moved thee to such hostility,
What made thee then the Fountain to forsake,
And unto broken Pits thyself betake?
What reason hadst thou to dishonor God,
Who thee with Mercies never ceas'd to load?
Because the Lord was good hast thou been evil,
And taken part against him with the Devil?
For all his cost to pay him with despite,
And all his love with hatred to requite?
Is this the fruit of God's great patience,
To wax more bold in disobedience?
To kick against the bowels of his Love?
Is this aright his Bounty to improve?
Stand still, ye Heav'ns, and be astonishéd,
That God by man should thus be injuréd!
Give ear, O Earth, and tremble at the sin
Of those that thine Inhabitants have been!
But thou, vile wretch, hast added unto all
Thine other faults and facts so criminal,
The damning sin of willful unbelief;
Of all Transgressors hast thou been the chief.
Yet when time was thou might'st have been set free
From Sin and Wrath and punishment by me;
But thou would'st not accept of Gospel Grace,
Nor on my terms Eternal Life embrace.
As if that all thy breaches of God's Law
Were not enough upon thy head to draw
Eternal Wrath, thou hast despis'd a Savior,
Rejected me, and trampled on my favor.
How oft have I stood knocking at thy door,

And been deniéd entrance evermore ?
How often hath my Spirit been withstood,
When as I sent him to have done thee good?
Thou hast no need of any one to plead
Thy cause or for thy Soul to intercede:
Plead for thyself, if thou hast aught to say,
And pay thy forfeiture without delay.
Behold thou dost ten thousand Talents owe;
Pay thou the debt or else to Prison go."

Think, think, O man, when Christ shall thus unfold
Thy secret guilt, and make thee to behold
The ugly face of all thy sinful errors,
And fill thy soul with his amazing terrors,
And let thee see the flaming Pit of Hell,
Where all that have no part in him shall dwell;
When he shall thus expostulate the case,
How canst thou bear to look him in the face ?
What wilt thou do without an Advocate,
Or plead, when thus thy state is desperate ?
Dost think to put him off with fair pretenses ?
Or wilt thou hide and cover thine offenses ?
Can anything from him concealéd be,
Who doth the hidden things of darkness see ?
Art thou of force his Power to withstand ?
Canst thou by might escape out of his hand ?
Dost thou intend to run out of his sight,
And save thyself from punishment by flight ?
Or wilt thou be eternally accurst,
And 'bide his Vengeance, let him do his worst ?
Oh ! who can bear his indignation's heat ?
Or 'bide the pains of Hell which are so great ?

If, then, thou neither canst his Wrath endure,
Nor any ransom after death procure;

If neither Cries nor Tears can move his heart
To pardon thee or mitigate thy smart,
But unto Hell thou must perforce be sent,
With dismal horror and astonishment,
Consider, O my Friend, what cause thou hast,
With fear and trembling (while as yet thou may'st),
To lay to heart thy sin and misery,
And to make out after the Remedy.
Consider well the greatness of thy danger,
O Child of wrath, and object of God's anger.
Thou hangest over the Infernal Pit,
By one small thread, and car'st not thou a whit?
There's but a step between thy Soul and Death;
Nothing remains but stopping of thy breath,
(Which may be done to-morrow, or before)
And then thou art undone forevermore.
Let this awaken thy security,
And make thee look about thee speedily.

How canst thou rest an hour or sleep a night,
Or in thy creature-comforts take delight?
Or with vain Toys thyself forgetful make
How near thou art unto the burning Lake?
How canst thou live without tormenting fears?
How canst thou hold from weeping floods of tears?
Yea, tears of blood, I might almost have said,
If such-like tears could from thine eyes be shed.
To gain the world what will it profit thee,
And lose thy soul and self eternally?
Eternity on one small point dependeth;
The man is lost that this short life misspendeth.
For as the Tree doth fall, right so it lies,
And man continues in what state he dies.
Who happy die shall happy rise again;

Who curséd die shall curséd still remain.
If under Sin and Wrath Death leaves thee bound,
At Judgment under Wrath thou shalt be found ;
And then woe woe that ever thou wert born,
O wretched man, of Heav'n and Earth forlorn !
Consider this, all ye that God forget,
Who all his threatenings at naught do set,
Lest into pieces he begin to tear
Your souls, and there be no deliverer.

O you that now sing care and fear away,
Think often of the formidable Day,
Wherein the Heavens with a mighty noise,
And with a hideous, heart-confounding voice
Shall pass away, together being roll'd,
As men are wont their garments up to fold;
When th' Elements with fervent heat shall melt,
And living Creatures in the same shall swelt,
And altogether in those flames expire,
Which set the Earth's Foundati-ons on fire.
Oh ! what amazements will your hearts be in,
And how will you to curse yourselves begin,
For all your damnéd sloth and negligence,
And unbelief and gross Impenitence,
When you shall hear that dreadful Sentence pass'd,
That all the wicked into Hell be cast !
What horrors will your Consciences surprise,
When you shall hear the fruitless, doleful cries
Of such as are compelléd to depart
Unto the place of everlasting smart !
What ! when you see the sparks fly out of Hell,
And view the Dungeon where you are to dwell,
Wherein you must eternally remain
In anguish and intolerable pain !
What ! when your hands and feet are bound together,

And you are cast into the Lake forever !
Then shall you feel the truth of what you hear,
That Hellish pains are more than you can bear,
And that those Torments are an hundred fold
More terrible than ever you were told.

Nor speak I this, good Reader, to torment thee
Before the time, but rather to prevent thee
From running headlong to thine own decay,
In such a perilous and deadly way.
We who have known and felt Jehovah's terrors,
Persuade men to repent them of their errors,
And turn to God in time ere his Decree
Bring forth, and then there be no Remedy.
If in the night, when thou art fast asleep,
Some friend of thine that better watch doth keep,
Should see thy house all on a burning flame,
And thee almost inclosed with the same :
If such a friend should break thy door and wake thee,
Or else by force out of the peril take thee,
What ! wouldst thou take his kindness in ill part,
Or frown upon him for his good desert ?

Such, O my friend, such is thy present state
And danger, being unregenerate.
Awake, awake, and then thou shalt perceive
Thy peril greater than thou wilt believe.
Lift up thine eyes, and see God's wrathful ire
Preparing unextinguishable fire
For all that live and die impenitent.
Awake, awake, O Sinner, and repent,
And quarrel not because I thus alarm
Thy Soul, to save it from eternal harm.

Perhaps thou harborest such thoughts as these :
"I hope I may enjoy my carnal case

A little longer, and myself refresh
With those delights that gratify the flesh,
And yet repent before it be too late,
And get into a comfortable state.
I hope I have yet many years to spend,
And time enough those matters to attend."
Presumptuous heart! Is God engag'd to give
A longer time to such as love to live
Like Rebels still, who think to strain his Glory
By wickedness, and after to be sorry ?
Unto thy lust shall he be made a drudge,
Who thee and all ungodly men shall judge ?
Canst thou account sin sweet, and yet confess
That first or last it ends in bitterness ?
Is sin a thing that must procure thee sorrow,
And wouldst thou dally with't another morrow ?

O foolish man who lovest to enjoy
That which will thee distress, or else destroy !
What gainéd Samson by his Delilah ?
What gainéd David by his Bathshebah ?
The one became a slave, lost both his eyes,
And made them sport that were his enemies ;
The other penneth, as a certain token
Of God's displeasure, that his bones were broken,
Besides the woes he after met withal,
To chasten him for that his grievous Fall :
His own Son Ammon, using crafty wiles,
His Daughter Thamar wickedly defiles :
His second Son, more beautiful than good,
His hands embreweth in his Brother's blood :
And by and by, aspiring to the Crown,
He strives to pull his gentle Father down ;
With hellish rage, him fiercely persecuting,
And brutishly his Concubines polluting.

Read whoso list, and ponder what he reads,
And he shall find small joy in evil deeds.

Moreover this consider, that the longer
Thou liv'st in sin, thy sins will grow the stronger;
And then it will an harder matter prove
To leave those wicked haunts that thou dost love.
The Black'moor may as eas'ly change his skin,
As old Transgressors leave their wonted sin.
And who can tell what will become of thee,
Or where thy Soul in one day's time may be ?
We see that Death ne'er old nor young men spares,
But one and other takes at unawares ;
For in a moment, whilst men Peace do cry,
Destruction seizeth on them suddenly.
Thou who this morning art a lively wight,
May'st be a corpse and damnéd Ghost ere night.

Oh ! dream not then that it will serve thy turn
Upon thy Death-bed for thy sins to mourn ;
But think how many have been snatch'd away,
And had no time for mercy once to pray.
It's just with God Repentance to deny
To such as put it off until they die.
And late Repentance seldom proveth true,
Which, if it fail, thou know'st what must ensue ;
For after this short life is at an end,
What is amiss thou never canst amend.
Believe, O man, that to procrastinate,
And put it off until it be too late,
As 'tis thy sin, so it is Satan's wile,
Whereby he doth great multitudes beguile.
How many thousands hath this strong delusion
Already brought to ruin and confusion,
Whose souls are now reserv'd in iron chains,

Under thick darkness to Eternal Pains !
They thought of many years, as thou dost now,
But were deceivéd quite, and so may'st thou.

Oh ! then, my friend, waste not away thy time,
Nor by rebellion aggravate thy crime.
Oh ! put not off Repentance till to-morrow,
Adventure not, without God's leave, to borrow
Another day to spend upon thy lust,
Lest God (that is most Holy, Wise, and Just)
Denounce in wrath, and to thy terror say,
" This night shall Devils fetch thy Soul away."

Now seek the face of God with all thy heart,
Acknowledge unto him how vile thou art.
Tell him thy Sins deserve eternal wrath,
And that it is a wonder that he hath
Permitted thee so long to draw thy breath,
Who might have cut thee off by sudden death,
And sent thy Soul into the lowest Pit,
From whence no price should ever ransom it ;
And that he may most justly do it still,
(Because thou hast deserv'd it) if he will.
Yet also tell him that, if he shall please,
He can forgive thy sins and thee release,
And that in Christ his Son he may be just
And justify all those that on him trust ;
That though thy sins are of a crimson dye,
Yet Christ his Blood can cleanse thee thoroughly.
Tell him that he may make his Glorious Name
More wonderful by covering thy shame ;
That Mercy may be greatly magnified,
And justice also fully satisfied,
If he shall please to own thee in his Son,
Who hath paid dear for Man's Redempti-on.

Tell him thou hast an unbelieving heart,
Which hind'reth thee from coming for a part
In Christ; and that although his terrors awe thee,
Thou canst not come till he be pleas'd to draw thee.
Tell him thou know'st thine heart to be so bad,
And thy condition so exceeding sad,
That though Salvation may be had for naught
Thou canst not come and take it till thou'rt brought.

Oh! beg of him to bow thy stubborn will
To come to Christ, that he thy lusts may kill.
Look up to Christ for his attractive pow'r,
Which he exerteth in a needful hour;
Who saith, "When as I lifted up shall be,
Then will I draw all sorts of men to me."
Oh! wait upon him with true diligence
And trembling fear in every Ordinance;
Unto his Call earnest attention give,
Whose voice makes deaf men hear and dead men live.
Thus weep and mourn, thus hearken, pray, and wait,
Till he behold and pity thine estate,
Who is more ready to bestow his Grace
Than thou the same art willing to embrace;
Yea, he hath Might enough to bring thee home,
Though thou hast neither strength nor will to come.

If he delay to answer thy request,
Know that ofttimes he doth it for the best;
Not with intent to drive us from his door,
But for to make us importune him more;
Or else to bring us daily to confess,
And be convinc'd of our unworthiness.
Oh! be not weary, then, but persevere
To beg his Grace till he thy suit shall hear;
And leave him not, nor from his footstool go,
Till over thee Compassion's skirt he throw.

Eternal Life shall recompense thy pains,
If found at last, with everlasting gains.
For if the Lord be pleas'd to hear thy cries,
And to forgive thy great iniquities,
Thou wilt have cause forever to admire
And laud his Grace, that granted thy desire.
Then shalt thou find thy labor is not lost,
But that the good obtain'd surmounts the cost.
Nor shalt thou grieve for loss of sinful pleasures,
Exchang'd for Heav'nly joys and lasting treasures.
The yoke of Christ which once thou didst esteem
A tedious yoke, shall then most easy seem.
For why ?   The love of Christ shall thee constrain
To take delight in that which was thy pain.
The ways of Wisdom shall be pleasant ways,
And thou shalt choose therein to spend thy days.

If once thy Soul be brought to such a pass,
O bless the Lord and magnify his Grace.
Thou that of late hadst reason to be sad,
May'st now rejoice and be exceeding glad ;
For thy condition is as happy now
As erst it was disconsolate and low.
Thou art become as rich, as whilom poor ;
As blesséd now as curséd heretofore.
For being cleanséd with Christ's precious Blood,
Thou hast an int'rest in the chiefest Good ;
God's anger is towards thy Soul appeas'd,
And in his Christ he is with thee well pleas'd.
Yea, he doth look upon thee with a mild
And gracious aspect, as upon his child.
He is become thy Father and thy Friend,
And will defend thee from the curséd Fiend.
Thou need'st not fear the roaring Lion's rage,
Since God Almighty doth himself engage

To bear thy Soul in everlasting Arms,
Above the reach of all destructive harms.
Whatever here thy sufferings may be,
Yet from them all the Lord shall rescue thee.
He will preserve thee by his wond'rous Might
Unto that rich Inheritance in Light.

O sing for joy, all ye Regenerate,
Whom Christ hath brought unto this blessed state !
O love the Lord all ye his saints, who hath
Redeeméd you from everlasting wrath !
Who hath by dying made your Souls to live,
And what he dearly bought doth freely give.
Give up yourselves to walk in all his ways,
And study how to live unto his praise.
The time is short you have to serve him here ;
The day of your deliv'rance draweth near.
Lift up your heads, ye upright ones in heart,
Who in Christ's purchase have obtain'd a part.
Behold he rides upon a shining cloud,
With angel's voice and Trumpet sounding loud.
He comes to save his folk from all their foes,
And plague the men that Holiness oppose.
So come, Lord Jesus, quickly come, we pray ;
Yea, come and hasten our Redemption-day.

VANITY OF VANITIES.

A SONG OF EMPTINESS.

VAIN, frail, short-liv'd, and miserable Man,
Learn what thou art when thy estate is best;
A restless Wave o' th' troubled Oce-an,
A Dream, a lifeless Picture finely drest.

A Wind, a Flower, a Vapor, and a Bubble, .
A Wheel that stands not still, a trembling Reed,
A trolling Stone, dry Dust, light Chaff, and Stubble,
A shadow of something but truly naught indeed.

Learn what deceitful Toys and empty things
This World and all its best Enjoyments be ;
Out of the Earth no true Contentment springs,
But all things here are vexing Vanity.

For what is Beauty but a fading Flower ?
Or what is Pleasure but the Devil's bait,
Whereby he catcheth whom he would devour,
And multitudes of Souls doth ruinate ?

And what are Friends but mortal men as we,
Whom Death from us may quickly separate ?
Or else their hearts may quite estrangéd be,
And all their love be turnéd into hate.

And what are Riches to be doted on ?
Uncertain, fickle, and ensnaring things ;
They draw men's Souls into Perditi-on,
And when most needed take them to their wings.

(107)

Ah! foolish man! that sets his heart upon
Such empty shadows, such wild Fowl as these,
That being gotten will be quickly gone,
And whilst they stay increase but his disease.

As in a Dropsy, drinking drought begets,
The more he drinks the more he still requires,
So on this World whoso affection sets,
As Wealth's increase, increaseth his desires.

O happy Man, whose portion is above,
Where Floods, where Flames, where Foes cannot be-
    reave him!
Most wretched Man that fixèd hath his love
Upon this World, that surely will deceive him!

For what is Honor? what is Sovereignty,
Whereto men's hearts so restlessly aspire?
Whom have they crownèd with Felicity?
When did they ever satisfy desire?

The Ear of Man with hearing is not fill'd;
To see new sights still coveteth the Eye;
The craving stomach, though it may be still'd,
Yet craves again without a new supply.

All Earthly things man's cravings answer not,
Whose little heart would all the World contain,
(If all the World should fall to one man's lot)
And notwithstanding empty still remain.

The Eastern Conqueror was said to weep
When he the Indian Oce-an did view,
To see his Conquest bounded by the Deep,
And no more Worlds remaining to subdue.

Who would that man in his Enjoyment bless,
Or envy him, or covet his Estate,
Whose gettings do augment his greediness,
And make his wishes more intemperate?

Such is the wonted and the common guise
Of those on Earth that bear the greatest sway;
If with a few the case be otherwise,
They seek a Kingdom that abides for aye.

Moreover they of all the Sons of Men
That rule, and are in highest Places set,
Are most inclin'd to scorn their Bretheren,
And God himself (without great Grace) forget.

For as the Sun doth blind the gazers' eyes,
That for a time they naught discern aright,
So Honor doth befool and blind the Wise,
And their own lustre 'reaves them of their sight.

Great are their Dangers, manifold their Cares,
Through which, whilst others sleep, they scarcely Nap,
And yet are oft surpriséd unawares,
And fall unwilling into Envy's Trap.

The mean Mechanic finds his kindly rest;
All void of fear sleepeth the Country Clown;
When greatest Princes often are distrest,
And cannot sleep upon their Beds of Down.

Could Strength or Valor men Immortalize,
Could Wealth or Honor keep them from decay,
There were some cause the same to Idolize,
And give the lie to that which I do say.

But neither can such things themselves endure,
Without the hazard of a change, one hour,
Nor such as trust in them can they secure
From dismal days, or Death's prevailing pow'r.

If Beauty could the Beautiful defend
From Death's dominion, then fair Absalom
Had not been brought to such a shameful end:
But fair and foul unto the Grave must come.

If Wealth or Scepters could Immortal make,
Then, wealthy Crœsus, wherefore art thou dead?
If Warlike force which makes the World to quake,
Then why is Julius Cæsar perishéd?

Where are the Scipio's Thunderbolts of War?
Renownéd Pompey, Cæsar's Enemy?
Stout Hannibal, Rome's Terror known so far?
Great Alexander, what's become of thee?

If Gifts and Bribes Death's favor might but win,
If Pow'r, if Force, or Threat'nings might it fray,
All these, and more had still surviving been;
But all are gone, for Death will have no Nay.

Such is this World, with all her Pomp and Glory;
Such are the men whom worldly eyes admire,
Cut down by time, and now become a Story,
That we might after better things aspire.

Go boast thyself of what thy heart enjoys,
Vain Man! triumph in all thy worldly Bliss:
Thy best Enjoyments are but Trash and Toys;
Delight thyself in that which worthless is.

Omnia prætereunt præter amare Deum.

DEATH EXPECTED AND WELCOMED.

WELCOME sweet Rest, by me so long Desir'd,
Who have with Sins and Griefs so long been tir'd;
And welcome Death, my Father's Messenger;
Of my Felicity the Hastener.

Welcome good Angels, who, for me distrest,
Are come to guard me to Eternal Rest.
Welcome, O Christ, who hast my Soul Redeem'd,
Whose Favor I have more than Life esteem'd.

Oh! do not now my sinful soul forsake,
But to thyself thy Servant gath'ring take.
Into thy Hands I recommend my Spirit,
Trusting through Thee Eternal Life t' inherit.

(111)

A FAREWELL TO THE WORLD.

Now Farewell, World, in which is not my Treasure;
I have in thee enjoy'd but little Pleasure.
And now I leave thee for a Better Place,
Where lasting Pleasures are, before Christ's face.

Farewell, ye Sons of Men, who do not savor
The things of God; who little prize his Favor.
Farewell, I say, with your Fool's Paradise,
Until the King of Terrors you surprise,
And bring you trembling to Christ's Judgment Seat,
To give Account of your Transgressions great.

Farewell, New England, which hast long enjoy'd
The Day of Grace, but hast most vainly toy'd
And trifled with the Gospel's glorious Light;
Thou may'st expect a dark Egyptian Night.

Farewell, young Brood and rising Generation,
Wanton and proud, ripe for God's Indignation,
Which neither you nor others can prevent,
Except in Truth you speedily repent.

Farewell, sweet Saints of God, Christ's little Number,
Beware lest ye through sloth securely slumber;
Stand to your Spir'tual Arms and keep your Watch,
Let not your Enemy you napping catch;
Take up your Cross, prepare for Tribulation,
Through which doth lie the way unto salvation.

Love Jesus Christ with all sincerity;
Eschew Will-worship and Idolatry.
Farewell, again, until we all appear
Before our Lord, a *Well-done* there to hear.

Farewell, ye faithful Servants of the Lord,
Painful dispensers of his Holy Word,
From whose Communion and Society
I once was kept through long infirmity.
This of my Sorrows was an aggravation;
But Christ be thankèd, through whose Mediation
I have at length obtainèd Liberty
To dwell with Soul-delighting Company,
Where many of our Friends are gone before,
And you shall follow with a many more.
Meanwhile stand fast, the Truth of God maintain,
Suffer for Christ, and great shall be your Gain.

Farewell, my natural Friends and dear Relations,
Who have my Trials seen and great Temptations;
You have no cause to make for me great Moan;
My Death to you is little Loss or none.
But unto me it is no little Gain,
For Death at once frees me from all my Pain.
Make Christ your greatest Friend, who never dies;
All other Friends are fading Vanities.
Make him your Light, your Life, your End, your All;
Prepare for Death, be ready for his Call.

Farewell, vile Body, subject to decay,
Which art with lingering sickness worn away;
I have by thee much Pain and Smart endur'd;
Great Grief of Mind hast thou to me procur'd;
Great Grief of Mind by being Impotent,
And to Christ's Work an awkward Instrument.

Thou shalt not henceforth be a clog to me.
Nor shall my Soul a Burthen be to thee.

Rest in thy Grave until the Resurrection,
Then shalt thou be revivéd in Perfection,
Endow'd with wonderful Agility,
Clothéd with Strength and Immortality ;
With shining Brightness gloriously array'd,
Like to Christ's glorious Body, glorious made.
Thus Christ shall thee again to me restore,
Ever to live with him and part no more.
Meanwhile my Soul shall enter into Peace,
Where Fears and Tears, where Sin and Smart shall cease.

A

CHARACTER

OF THE REVEREND AUTHOR,

Mr. MICHAEL WIGGLESWORTH,

IN A FUNERAL SERMON PREACHED AT

MALDEN, JUNE 24, 1705.

BY THE REVEREND DR. COTTON MATHER.

HE was Descended of Eminently Religious Parents, who were Sufferers for that which was then *The Cause of God* and of *New-England.* While he was yet a youth, he was marvellously concerned that he might have an Heart filled with the Spirit of God. This Concernment upon his mind.appeared especially in his watchful Endeavors to have *Spiritual Sins* chased out of his cleansed Heart. PRIDE, the Sin of *Young Men,* yea, of *all* Men ; PRIDE, the Sin which few Men try or trouble themselves about ; this Devout Youth was full of Holy and Watchful Trouble about it : And he then wrote a very Savoury Discourse, Entituled, *Considerations against Pride,* and another, Entituled, *Considerations against Delighting more in the Creature than in God.* This was to Mortify in himself the Sins rarely minded by the most of men.

Having had a Pious and a Learned Education, the first Publick Station wherein I find him, was that of a *Fellow* and a *Tutor* in *Harvard Colledge.* With a rare Faithful-

115)

ncss did he adorn that Station! IIe used all means
imaginable to make his *Pupils* not only good Scholars,
but also good *Christians*, and instil into them those
things which might render them rich Blessings unto the
Churches of God. Unto his Watchful and Painful Essays
to keep them close under their *Academical Exercises*, he
added Serious Admonitions unto them about their Inte-
rior State; and he Employed his *Prayers* and *Tears* to
God for them, and had such a flaming zeal to make
them worthy Men, that upon Reflection he was afraid
*Lest his cares for their Good, and his affection to them, should
so drink up his very Spirit, as to steal away his Heart from
God.*

From *Cambridge* he made his remove to *Malden*, and
was their Faithful Pastor for about a Jubilee of years
together.

It was not long after his coming to Malden that a sickly
Constitution so prevailed upon him, as to confine him
from his Publick Work for some whole seven of Years.
IIis *Faithfulness* continued when his *Ministry* was thus
interrupted. The Kindness of his Tender Flock unto
him was answered in his Kind Concern to have them
served by other Hands. He took a short voyage unto
another Country for the Recovery of his Health; which,
though he recovered not, yet at his Return I find him
comforting himself with inserting of this Passage in his
Reserved Papers:

Peradventure the Lord Removed me for a season that he might
set a better Watchman over his Flock, and a more painful La-
borer in his Vineyard. This was one thing that I aimed at in
Removing (to help the People's Modesty in the case), and I believe
the Lord aimed at it, in Removing me for a season.

His Faithfulness now appeared in his *Edifying Dis-
courses* to those that came near him; much bewailing

the want of a Profitable and Religious conversation in so many that profess Religion. And that yet he might more *Faithfully* set himself to do Good, when he could not Preach he *Wrote* several Composures, wherein he proposed the edification of such Readers as are for plain Truths, dressed up in a *Plain Meeter*. These Composures have had their Acceptance and Advantage among that sort of Readers ; and one of them, the *Day of Doom*, which has been often Reprinted in both *Englands*, may find our Children till the *Day* itself arrive.

It pleased God, when the distress of the Church in *Malden* did extremely call for it, wondrously to restore his *Faithful Servant*. He that had been for near Twenty Years almost *Buried Alive*, comes abroad again, and for as many years more, must, in *Publick Usefulness*, receive the Answer and Harvest of the Thousands of Supplications with which the *God of his Health* had favoured him.

How *Faithfully* did he now Deliver the *Whole Counsel of God !*

How *Faithfully* did he Rebuke *Sin*, both in his *Ministry* and *Discipline !*

How Faithful was he to the *Work of God* in the Churches of *New-England*, and grieved at every thing that he thought had any Tendency to incommode that Glorious Work ! But how *Patient*, how *Loving*, how *Charitable* to such as in lesser Matters differed from him !

How Faithful was he in the Education of his *Family !* A very Abraham for his Commands unto them, to *Keep the Way of the Lord !* A very David for his charge unto them to *Know the God of their Father and Serve Him !*

His long Weakness and Illness made him an *able Physician* for the *Body* as well the *Soul*.

As he was *Faithful to the Death*, so he was *Lively to the Death*.

It was a surprise to us to see a little, feeble *Shadow*

of a Man, beyond *Seventy,* Preaching usually twice or thrice in a week, Visiting, Comforting the *Afflicted,* Encouraging the *Private Meetings, Catechising* the Children of the Flock, and managing the *Government* of the Church, and attending the *Sick,* not only as a *Pastor,* but as a *Physician* too ; and this not only in his own Town, but also in all those of the Vicinity.   Thus he did *unto the Last ;* and he was but one *Lord's-Day* taken off before his Last.   But in the *Last Week* of his Life, how full of *Resignation !*   How full of *Satisfaction !*

From his Exemplary Life I will single out one thing, his EARLY RELIGION.   Our *Wigglesworth* was a Godly child, and he held on living to God and Christ until the Seventy-Fourth Year of his Age.

When he lay a Dying, some one spoke to him about his having secured his *Interest* in the Favor of Heaven, and his *Assurance* of that Interest.   He Replyed, [Methoughts like my *Polycarp,*]

I bless God I began that Work betimes, and ere I was Twenty Years Old I had made thorow work of it.   Ever since then I have been pressing after the Power of Godliness, the Power of Godliness !   For more than Fifty Years together I have been Laboring to uphold a Life of Communion with God ; and I thank the Lord I now find the Comfort of it !

Words that contain in them *A History of a Life* more Valuable than I have seen a Volume in Folio.

EPITAPH.

(BELIEVED TO HAVE BEEN WRITTEN BY REV. COTTON MATHER.)

THE EXCELLENT
WIGGLESWORTH;
REMEMBERED BY SOME GOOD TOKENS.

His Pen did once *Meat from the Eater* fetch;
And now he's gone beyond the *Eater's* reach.
His *Body* once so *Thin*, was next to *None;*
From hence he's to *Unbodied Spirits* flown.
Once his rare skill did all *Diseases* heal;
And he does nothing now *uneasy* feel.
He to his *Paradise* is joyful come,
And waits with joy to see his *Day of Doom.*
(119)

CONTENTS.

—•◆•—